Foolish

Foolish

Anna Black

www.urbanbooks.net

Urban Books, LLC
300 Farmingdale Road, NY-Route 109
Farmingdale, NY 11735

ISBN 13: 978-1-945855-74-0
ISBN 10: 1-945855-74-6

First Mass Market Printing December 2018
First Trade Paperback Printing February 2018
Printed in the United States of America

10 9 8 7 6 5 4 3 2 1

Distributed by Kensington Publishing Corp.
Submit orders to:
Customer Service
400 Hahn Road
Westminster, MD 21157-4627
Phone: 1-800-733-3000
Fax: 1-800-659-243

Prologue

"Luck" would have never been a word used when describing November's life, unless the word "bad" was in front of it. No matter how she tried or what she did, she always caught hell for some reason or another. She didn't have a clue as to what she had done that was so evil it had caused her a laundry list of incidents. There was situation after situation, and she figured it had something to do with one of her past lives.

She was easygoing, levelheaded, and she always tried to see the good in all things and situations. She trusted and believed in God, and she didn't know why He kept putting her through so much. She wasn't a big churchgoing person, so her momma always commented that that was why she was catching hell. However, she knew in her heart that wasn't true. She had a few slips here and there, of course, but she repented and always tried to stay on the straight and narrow.

"God, please tell me why my car has to be totaled," she said after she hung up with the insurance appraiser. She was just getting herself established after the hellish ride of college and graduate school, and her car being totaled was the last thing she needed.

She had made it through the evil, lying, scheming roommates, and the back and forth of living with her parents. Then there was the series of boyfriends who were hounds and nutcases. She'd thought after all she had been through, God would cut her some slack, but no, she was facing yet another dilemma.

She had finally gotten a piece of her own independence, and things were slowly but definitely changing for her. Her new job was going well. Her very old one-bedroom matchbox of an apartment was going to be a thing of the past in about nine weeks, because she was planning to close on her first condo. But then what? Her car was totaled. She was happy that she was alive and able to walk away from the accident unharmed—and she knew to thank God for that—but why there was obstacle after obstacle for her to overcome was beyond her.

"I can't make it in this city without a car." She huffed, dreading that she was going to have to be on the bus. Not that CTA was an awful service; she just didn't want to have to be on the bus.

She worked downtown, so going to work was a breeze on the train, but her social life—not that she had a great one—would be impossible without her own transportation.

November was stuck. She thought about asking her daddy to sign for a car until after the closing, but after the million favors he had already done in the past, she didn't want to open her mouth again to ask him for more help.

That was one of the reasons she was living in a one-bedroom dump. She was trying to finish school and not ask her parents for anything if she could avoid it. When she was living with them, she detested going home, because they were a holier-than-thou couple and it drove her insane. So, when she had the opportunity to move, she moved into her own place. Once she graduated and started working, she knew she wanted to buy a home, so she dealt with her living conditions long enough to save some money to get her new condo. She also had to establish work history, so she waited until after her second year at the company to look for her place.

Her parents were disappointed that she'd rather live in that awful, horrible apartment instead of living with them. Her daddy asked her 5,000 times to allow him to get her another place and help her with her bills, but she had insisted that she'd do things for herself for a change. Her parents had carried her for too long, and she wanted to finally have her freedom and independence. If her daddy would have been the one to get her a place, he would have wanted to monitor everything she did. Just like he did when she was living at home with them.

She just could not take it anymore with her parents. Her daddy would screen her calls and interrogate her dates as if she were still sixteen. He even told one of her dates not to bring her home too late. At the time, she was in her last year of undergrad. That was when she had to go, because a sister couldn't get any action or keep a man while living with those two. If she stayed at a guy's place to try to get her a piece for a few days, they'd be at the door ready to kick her out, because they still wanted to treat her like a child.

"God, why now? Why couldn't my car make it to the day after I close? Why am I in yet another situation, Lord Jesus? Please give me an answer," she prayed.

In a couple of days, she had to return the rental. After that, she would be on public transportation because she had no choice or any other options. She wished she at least had a boyfriend who could get her around, but she was single and alone, with no prospects.

Now she was where she hated to be: in tears. November felt that disaster always had a way of striking in her life. No matter what it was, she could never see herself in anything perfect or nondramatic. When good things happened to her, like being able to walk away from a wreck without a scratch, she knew that God was with her. When she walked out of the hospital after the doctor released her with a clean bill of health, she looked up to the sky and winked at God. She knew He had spared her life to see how much more she could bear.

Part One

Chapter One

"Thank you, sir," November said, getting out of the passenger side of the Enterprise rental car. It was two weeks after the wreck and her final day of having a set of wheels. Now that the rental car was returned, she had no transportation.

The clerk had dropped her off at the towing company so she could get her personal belongings from her busted-up Honda Accord. Her daddy had given her that car as a gift on the day she graduated college. It was paid in full with only 51,000 miles on it. She loved that car. It had treated her so well, and the thought of having a car note made her angry. She already had enough on her plate. God was surely making it hard for her, she thought as she watched the rental car drive away.

She opened the gate and walked into the trailer looking for someone to help her, but she didn't see anyone. "Hello," she yelled.

When no one responded, she walked over to the little window to see if she could spot anyone, but instead, her eyes landed on her beat-up car. Her baby was over to the left side of the tow yard, looking so pitiful. She felt like a part of her was gone.

She walked back out the door to look around outside, and she saw a tall man walking around with a clipboard in his hand. As he got closer, she could see his tanned complexion and muscular arms. She still couldn't see his face from where she was standing, but she could see his blue uniform and black steel-toed boots. Realizing that she had been watching him for a few minutes, she walked down the trailer steps to get his attention.

"Hey, hello," she yelled. He didn't look her way, so she guessed he didn't hear her. "Hey," she yelled again, "are you the only one here?"

He turned to her. "Give me a moment, ma'am," he yelled back.

He started to walk in her direction. His long strides closed the distance between them in a matter of seconds. As he got closer, she could see how good-looking he was. He had nice brown skin and thick eyebrows. His lashes were long, and he had a goatee that looked good on him. When he reached her, she could see he was well over six feet.

"Hey, I am sorry, ma'am. I didn't see anyone pull up, so I didn't know you were here," he said.

She followed him up the steps and allowed him to open the door for her. "Oh, it's okay. I was dropped off by someone."

"I see. How can I help you?"

"Well, I was told by my insurance company that I can get my personal belongings out of my car."

"Okay, give me a moment." He walked around to the other side of the counter to the computer. "This will just take a second. You can have a seat if you'd like," he offered. She continued to stand at the counter instead of sitting on the vinyl sofa. "Your name?" he asked.

"Shareese . . . I mean, November. November McKinney."

"November McKinney," he repeated as he typed. "And the year, make, and model of your car?"

"2014 Honda Accord."

"Okay, here it is." He reached over to a board that hung on the wall behind the counter with dozens of keys hanging on it. He grabbed one. "Come on, follow me." He headed for the door, and she followed him out to her beat-up piece of steel. He opened the door and stepped out of her way. "Here you are, Mrs. McKinney," he said, giving her the key.

"It's Miss, and thank you, Tracy," she said, reading the name on his uniform shirt.

"No problem. Do you need help with anything?"

"No, I'll be fine. I don't have much. Everything should fit in my gym bag in the trunk."

"Okay, but if you need me, I'll be inside." He turned and walked away.

She emptied the glove box and got her white heart-shaped pillow from the back seat, stuffing it and her CDs and other items into the unused gym bag that had been in her trunk for more than a year. She shook her head. She hadn't been to the gym in ages. As a result, her size-fourteen booty was just a cheeseburger away from becoming a size sixteen.

After saying her last good-byes to the Accord, she headed back to the trailer with the bag. When she got inside, Tracy had a form for her to sign.

He handed her a pen. "Just sign here and initial here for me, and you are good."

She did as he instructed and handed the pen back to him. He looked over the document to verify her signature, she guessed, and put it in a file.

"Umm, how much longer will you be open?" she asked. "I need to call a cab."

"A cab?" he said.

"Yes, a cab," she repeated.

"How far are you going?"

"To Ninety-fifth. I can get the train from there."

"Well, I'm closing up now, and I'll be leaving in about ten minutes. I'd be happy to give you a ride."

"Oh, no worries. I'll be fine."

"November, come on. You know how much a cab is gonna cost from here to Ninety-fifth?"

"Yeah, a lot, I'm sure, but I'll be cool. And please don't call me that," she said with a frown.

"Call you what? November?" He tilted his head. "That is your name, right?"

"Yeah, but call me Shareese."

"Why? What's wrong with November?" He smiled.

"It's a stupid name and a stupid thing for a mother to do to her kid. To name your child after the month they were born in is crazy."

"No, I think it is cool. And November is a cool month. Just think about it. It could have been a month like February." He chuckled. She didn't laugh with him, so he stopped. "I think November is a cool name," he said awkwardly.

"Well, I don't. My mom, being as crazy as she is, named my sister April because that is the month when she was born, and then she turned around and named me November. That month being my birthday month made me grow up with a stupid name." She scrolled through her phone, looking for the nearest cab company.

"Look, November is an awesome month. That is the month I was born in, and I think that name suits you."

"Yeah, whatever," she said and clicked her tongue.

She paused the conversation with Tracy and called the cab company. Tracy went into his office and came out with a set of keys in hand. Disappointment rained over her face when they said it would be a wait of forty to fifty minutes. The tow company was going to be closing in ten minutes. She hung up the phone and looked up at the ceiling. Why was God so cruel to her? How was she going to wait at a closed tow company, all alone, for almost an hour?

Tracy walked around the counter. "I just need to shut down the computer. You call for your cab?"

"Yeah, but they will be fifty minutes," she said softly.

"Listen, November, I'm closing. I can get you to Ninety-fifth or even to your house," he said, offering her a ride again.

"Ninety-fifth will be cool," she said with a half smile. She called and cancelled the cab and waited for him to close up. "Thanks, Tracy," she said as they went out the back door.

He helped her into the passenger seat of a very nice Infiniti truck. She was relieved that his vehicle didn't look like one of the wrecks in the yard.

"So, what day is your birthday?" he asked.

Snatched from her thoughts, she turned to him with a small smile. "November twenty-ninth."

"No way!"

"Yes, way," she confirmed.

"For real, for real?"

She looked at him with an eyebrow raised. "Yes, for real." She wondered why he was so surprised. Why would she lie about her birthday?

"That is my birthday," he said.

"Stop lying," she said. No way could they have the same birthday. She never met anyone with the same birthday as hers.

"I'm serious."

Unconvinced, she said, "Let me see your ID."

He opened the armrest, pulled out his driver's license, and handed it to her. It was true. Tracy Lamar Stone had been born on her birthday.

"Wow, Tracy, this is bizarre. I have never met anyone with the same birthday as mine."

"Same year too?" he asked.

"No, I'm a year older, but wow," she said and handed him his ID back.

"So, where do you live?" he asked.

"On Sixty-fourth," she said and turned to look out the window.

"Oh, I can take you home if you'd like. I have to go past Sixty-fourth to go home."

"No, Ninety-fifth is fine. I don't wanna put you out," she said. Although a ride would have been great, the truth was she didn't want him to see where she lived.

"No, it's fine. I have to pass Sixty-fourth, November," he insisted.

Finally, she agreed. It wasn't like she was going to see him again. "Okay, thank you." She looked at him. He was beautiful, she thought. When he looked at her, she turned forward quickly. She hated he had caught her checking him out. "Where do you live?" she asked.

"In the West Loop area, on Thirty-fifth near LaSalle."

"Really? I'm in the process of buying a condo in that area. I close in about seven weeks, near Park Alexandria."

"That's cool. I know the area. That's not too far from me. Congrats."

"Thanks. That is about the only good thing I've got going for myself right now. I need a car, but you know, no car 'til closing."

"Yeah, I know. I feel for you. That has to suck."

"It does, but what can I do, right?"

"Yes, you're right."

"So, why do you live so far from your job?"

"Well, that is my new location. I have another, Stone Cold Towing, on Thirty-first and Michigan."

"Oh, so you own the towing company?"

"Yes. When my pops passed, I inherited the business. I opened the new location about a year ago. I'm working farther out at the new location to get it going. Store number one is doing really well without me being there every day. That one is popular, got a lot of contracts, so I'm trying to build business out this way."

"Oh, okay."

She gave him directions to her dreadful apartment. They rode in silence until they reached her place.

"So, Ms. November," Tracy said when he parked, "again, congrats on your new place, and if you ever need any towing services, just call me." He handed her a card.

"Thanks, Tracy. And again, please call me Shareese."

He smiled at her. "No, I like November."

"Fine, if that works for you," she said and shut the door. She walked up the sidewalk to the building, and he pulled off.

As usual, meddlesome Ms. Wanda was in her window with a Newport dangling from her mouth. "Hey, I see you finally got a man," she belted.

"Hey, Ms. Wanda. And that is not my man, so mind your business."

"Don't tell me to mind my business. My business is this building, and you, my dear, live in this building."

"Ms. Wanda, you are the landlord. Your business is this building, not what I do or who I do it with."

"Don't get smart, Miss Thang. You know I can put you out before your little notice date."

"Yes, you can, Ms. Wanda, and I can also sue you for breach of contract."

That shut the older woman up quick, but she rolled her eyes. She was so simple she didn't remember the lease had expired more than three months ago. November was living month to month without any type of lease.

"Well, one thing is for sure, Ms. Shareese: your new man pushing some nice wheels." Ms. Wanda smiled.

To keep from carrying on any more conversation, November agreed and walked into the building.

She took off her jacket and went into her tiny kitchen to get a snack. She wasn't hungry, but she wanted to munch. She hit the speaker-phone button and dialed into her voice mail. She looked at the card that Tracy had given her, and she realized she had left her bag on the floor in the tow yard trailer. "Damn," she said. "How could I be so simple to forget my bag?"

After she listened to her messages, she dialed the cell number on the card. When voice mail answered, she hung up. After she showered, she tried calling him again, this time from her cell phone. Her home number was blocked. Maybe he didn't answer calls from private numbers.

He answered on the third ring. "Hello." She heard the volume of his music go down.

"Hello, Tracy, this is Shareese."

"Shareese?" he said as if the name were not familiar.

"November."

"Oh, okay. What's up?"

"I know you may think I'm a little on the simple side."

"Why would I think that?"

"Because I forgot my bag. I left it in the trailer on the floor by the counter."

"Yes, November, you are by far the simplest woman I have ever met."

Her mouth dropped open, and her eyes widened. She could not believe he had actually said that to her. She was speechless.

"I . . . I," she stuttered. She didn't expect him to agree with her.

"November, I'm kidding. I'm joking. I can bring it to you tomorrow after I am done working."

She let the air out of her chest. "Man, I was gon' say," she said.

"You know I was just joking. I will swing by there tomorrow with your bag, okay?"

"Are you sure? I don't want to put you out. I wouldn't have a problem coming by to get it, but you know I am without a vehicle."

"No, it's no problem. I got you," he said.

His voice was soothing, and she could tell that he was cool with it, so she agreed. "Thanks, Tracy. I will give you gas money for doing that for me."

"November, please. Don't insult me. I'll be all right. Plus, I may have an offer for you."

She flopped down onto the sofa. "What kind of an offer?"

"Something that may help you out. We can talk about it tomorrow when I come over to bring your bag."

She frowned. "Okay," she said slowly.

"Cool. Talk to you later."

"Okay," she said and hung up the phone. *What could he possibly have to offer me?*

She got up and headed for the kitchen, where she grabbed cheese from the fridge and popped a cube into her mouth. Then she went for the red wine and a glass and spent the rest of the night wondering what was on Tracy's mind.

Chapter Two

The next day, November got up and went to the bank to deposit her insurance check. She then grabbed a cab and went to check out a couple of furniture stores, checking out what was new and hot. None of that old college thrift-store mess was going into her new place, she thought as she walked through the stores. After the last store, she hopped on the bus and headed back to the Ninety-fifth Street train station and rode back to her place. By the time she got home, the sun was going down, and she was exhausted from the hustle and bustle of her day. She ate her Italian beef sandwich and decided to do a little work around the house. She put her iPod on the dock and got busy while she listened to Mary J. Blige.

She had already begun packing, so she had boxes all over. She took a shower, then sat on the couch with a glass of merlot. The music was good and the evening breeze from the window was nice. Strangely, her block was quiet, which was totally out of the ordinary for a Saturday night. Someone was always out or yelling from their windows, but that night, no one was moving around.

Her cell phone rang, and she looked at the caller ID. The number wasn't familiar, but she answered it anyway, thinking she'd hang up if it was someone she didn't want to talk to.

"Hello," she said, her voice low. She wasn't sure why she did that, but she figured it must have been the merlot.

"November?" a male voice said.

"Yes?" she answered, wondering who in the hell was calling her that.

"Hey, this is Trey."

She had no idea who Trey was. "Who?" she asked suspiciously.

"Tracy. Tracy Stone from Stone Cold Towing."

"Oh, hey, Tracy. What's up?"

"I am close to your place. Is it cool for me to bring your bag over?"

She had totally forgotten he was coming by to bring her bag. "Oh, I forgot." She looked down at the dingy old sweats she had on and sprang from the sofa.

"Is this not a good time?"

"Oh, no, you're fine. I just forgot, but it's okay for you to come."

"Okay, I'll be there in about thirty minutes."

"Okay. You know what building, right?"

"The one on the right?"

"Yeah. I'm in building C, apartment C3."

"Okay. I'll see you soon."

"Okay," she said.

Thanking God Tracy had said thirty minutes, she hung up, and she dashed into the bathroom. She removed her scarf, applied a little of her MAC gloss, and sprayed on some cherry blossom body spray. Then she threw on a pair of capris and a Supergirl T-shirt. After lighting a couple candles and moving a few boxes to the side, she thought her place still wasn't ready for company. She hardly ever had anyone over, so the boxes had never been a big concern for her. She hoped he'd chalk the mess up to her moving soon.

As soon as she refilled her glass, she heard a knock at the door. She knew it was Tracy, but she looked through the peephole anyway. When she opened the door, she was pleasantly surprised to see him looking better than the night before. Instead of wearing the old blue uniform, he was dressed in a button-down shirt with a pair of jeans and white tennis shoes. His haircut was fresh with a nice, tight lining. He smiled, and she automatically smiled back at him.

"Hello," he said.

After a few seconds, she realized she hadn't invited him in. "Hey, come on in," she said, moving from in front of the door.

"Here is your bag." He handed it to her.

"Oh, thank you." She put it to the side.

"What's in that little bag? It's kinda heavy."

"Well, it's my CDs and other crap from my car. My workout clothes—or I should say unused workout clothes—are in there too. I have not used those in over a year. Why I still carried them, I have no clue."

"Workout? Girl, you are fine. What do you mean workout?" He eyed her up and down, and she knew he was examining her round hips, thick thighs, and plump ass. "In my opinion, you're perfectly fine. Thick, slim waist, and . . ." He cleared his throat.

"And what?"

"Let's just say you don't need the gym."

"I disagree. I can stand to lose some weight and get back into my clothes." She was well aware that her jeans were fitting her tighter.

"Well, you're doing just fine from where I'm standing."

"I'm sorry," she said, realizing they were still standing near the door. "Would you like to have a seat?"

"Sure," he said.

She extended an arm toward the sofa. "Can I get you a drink?"

"Yes, that would be nice. What do you have?"

"What do you drink? My liquor cart is stocked, from a few parties I've hosted for the people in my building. I have rum, vodka, wine, beer."

"I'll have a beer."

"Is Corona fine? That's all I have."

"Yeah, that is cool," he said.

She went into the kitchen to get it. As she opened the top, she couldn't help but wonder what was going on with Tracy. What kind of offer did he have? When she got back into the living room, he was relaxed on the sofa.

She handed him the beer. "Here you go." She got a coaster and joined him on the sofa with her glass of merlot.

"So, I see you're packing already."

"Yes. I am too, too excited to not pack."

"Yeah, I feel ya." He took a swallow of his beer. "When I got my loft, I was packed the same day I was approved for the mortgage. All I had to do was get a truck on closing day. Of course, then I only had a few items, because I was rooming with two of my partners for a whole minute before getting my own spot. So I had to basically start from scratch with furniture and everything."

"Yeah, I know what you mean. Been through the roommates, the dorms, and the living with my parents. And thank God I'm finally getting out of this dump. As soon as I move, I'm getting all new stuff myself, starting with a new car. Man, I can't wait to get me another car."

"Oh, yeah, the car. That is what I wanted to talk to you about. I may be able to help you out."

"Help me out how?"

"With your car situation."

She frowned. "How can you help me with that?"

"Well, as you know, we have two towing companies."

"Yeah," she said, still confused. *Who is "we"?* she wondered.

"Back when my daddy first started our first towing company, he used to do repos for loan companies. Business grew due to so many cars being repossessed, so my daddy decided he'd buy the cars from the loan companies at a lower price. After a while of doing that, he started a small used car dealership.

"Years later, of course, we have grown, and my brother, Trent, owns and runs our dealership. So, since you are in no position to finance a loan right now, I can get him to let you hold something 'til you close on your new place."

She tilted her head, blinked about ten times, and said, "You're kidding, right?"

He shook his head. "No, I'm serious."

She thought it was odd that a complete stranger was offering to give her a car on loan. "You're pulling my leg. This must be a joke." She waited for him to laugh or do something to show her that he was playing a trick.

"No," he said. His tone sounded as if it were obvious he was serious.

"What's the catch? I mean, you don't know me from a can of paint, and you'd trust me with a car from your family's lot?"

"November, I'm only trying to help you out. There is no catch, and this is not a gimmick. I don't do this every day. It's just, last night when I dropped you off, you seemed down about your car situation, and from the looks of your Accord, you took care of it. So, if you'd like to get a car to get around until you close on your condo, I would like to help you out." He shrugged. "If you don't need my help, just say so."

She fought to hold in her laughter because she was sure it was a joke. She still didn't believe his offer. "Look, Tracy—"

"Trey," he said. "I go by Trey. Everyone calls me Trey, not Tracy."

"Tracy," she said. She preferred it like he preferred November. "I appreciate your offer, but I'd hate to get a car from you and something happens to it. I don't know you well, and I'd be uneasy taking that type of risk."

"Well, November, we can get insurance on the car in your name, and you won't be without transportation. Listen, I know it's a strange offer, but I'm serious. I wanna help you out. No strings."

"Well, Tracy, I appreciate your offer, I really do, but I would like to think about it. I mean, I never expected you to offer me something this huge. I do appreciate you trying to help me out and all, but I just need to think about it."

He gave her a sexy smile. "Okay, cool, if that is your answer. Just know I'd like to help you."

"I know," she said, returning the smile.

They sat for hours, drinking, laughing, and telling stories to each other about family and college experiences.

She yawned and realized it was after three a.m., but she was enjoying his company so much she didn't want him to leave. He was just so funny and interesting, and she was having a good time with him. She really relished having him over, and she hated the idea of their night coming to an end.

"Are you tired?" he asked.

"Yeah, a little, but I'm good." She hoped he wanted to stay longer, because she didn't want him to leave.

He stood. "Can I use your bathroom?"

"Yeah, sure. It's around the corner, straight ahead." She gave him a point in the right direction, and he went down the hall into the bathroom.

While he was gone, she got their empty glasses and took them into the kitchen. He came into the kitchen as she was rinsing them in the sink.

"Well, Ms. November, I see it's pretty late, so I'll go so you can get some shut-eye."

"Okay. Hold on. I'll walk you out." She dried her hands with a paper towel.

"No, no, no. It's late, and if you walk me out, who's gonna walk you back in?" They both laughed.

"Aww, man, I'll be fine. This is my building and everyone knows me, so don't worry," she said.

She followed him to the door. When they got there, they stood for a moment in an awkward silence.

"You are a beautiful woman, November," Tracy said. He caressed her cheek.

"You think so?" she replied shyly. She did think she was cute, but the compliment coming from a man as fine as Tracy was a first. She didn't want to even imagine him being interested in her, because she knew she'd be setting herself up for failure. Guys like him never, ever went for her. Not in a million years would she get a date with someone so good-looking, she thought.

"Yes, I think so, and even if you decide not to use the car, I'd like it if you'd call me anyway," he said.

"Okay, I'll do that," she said.

She walked him out. He headed down the stairs, and she leaned over the banister and gave him another, "Good night."

"Good night, November," he responded. She stood in the hall until she heard the downstairs door shut.

"November? Who in the hell is November?" It was one of her nosy neighbors.

Before slamming her door, she said, "Mind your business, Roderick." She let out a breath. "Oooh, I can't wait to move outta this building!"

Chapter Three

"So, what do you think, April?" November asked. She had called to tell her sister about Tracy and his car offer.

"I think this is destiny."

"You say the craziest shit, April. Everything is destiny to you and your crazy momma. Born in April, so name her April. Born in November, so call her November. You and your momma are crazy."

"First of all, little sista, that is your momma too. And secondly, you don't think that this is destiny to meet a man with the same birthday as yours? Come on, this is phenomenal."

"You know what, Cleo?" Ever since that fake woman back in the nineties was on television with her fake Jamaican accent, November would always say that was going to be April one day, somewhere or on TV lying to people about their futures. "You are crazy. All I wanna know is do you think I should use the car, not how our meeting is destiny."

"And again, I say yes. You don't have a car, and
you can't finance anything or tamper with your
credit 'til you close. So, yes, receive your blessing
and move on."

November was still unsure. "You really think
I should?"

"For the hundredth time, deaf girl, yes," April
said, making her sister laugh. "I have a daycare
center to run, and I don't have time to keep
repeating myself. I swear you are slower than
some of these two-year-olds I got up in here."

"Okay then, April, get back to your brats. I will
talk to you later."

"Okay. Bye."

They hung up, and November sat in her office
wondering what she should do. She did have
one other option. She could just rent a car using
the money she had gotten from the insurance
company.

But when she went online to price car rentals
for the amount of time she would need it, it was
way more expensive than what she wanted to
spend. She had gotten a little more than $7,000
back, but she decided to use that money to buy
new furniture instead. She would be financing
a new car, so to not have to finance new furniture too would be a burden off of her bank
account.

She had no clue what to do. It was Tuesday, and she hadn't spoken to Tracy since Saturday night. She watched the clock tick and thought about him. She smiled to herself when she replayed his voice in her mind, hearing him say, "You are a beautiful woman." She couldn't help but wonder if he, in fact, meant what he said or if he was just talking out the side of his neck. She closed her eyes, remembering the soft touch of him caressing her face.

"Stop it. Don't even go there," she said out loud, snapping herself out of it. He couldn't be interested in her. *You'd only end up hurt,* she told herself, and she got back to work.

She fought the urge to call him, although she really wanted to take him up on his offer. Getting up an hour early to make it to work on time was killing her.

Her ride on the train was horrible. There were no seats until three stops before it was time to get off and her feet were aching. She had on her tennis shoes, but since she wasn't used to doing a lot of walking, the bottoms of her feet burned. After the last bus she had a two-block walk, so her shirt was stuck to her back from sweat. Her hair was glued to her forehead, and she just wanted to shower away the day and put her feet up.

When she finally made it home that evening, the sun was going down. "Damn, I miss my car," she said as she climbed the steps in her building. She got inside and headed straight for the shower. Then she settled on the sofa with a glass of wine to watch a little television.

The next morning, the beeping of her alarm jerked her out of her sleep. She sat up and realized that she had fallen asleep on the sofa. Her neck hurt from the odd position she'd slept in, but she had to go to work. She didn't want to take time off, because she was saving all of her personal, vacation, and sick days to move and get settled in.

She made a mad dash to the shower and put on something quick so she could get to the bus stop.

Although she ran almost a block, she still missed her bus and had to wait for the next one, and when the next one came, the bus didn't stop, because it was full. She winced and peered down the street, praying that another was close, but it was ten whole minutes before she was sitting next to a woman with a cranky baby. She was by the window, and she prayed that the woman would proceed, but she flopped down in the seat next to her.

Running late for work with no time to get her morning coffee, November wanted to gag the temperamental child who squirmed in his mother's lap. By the time she got onto the train, there was again standing room only. She hiked the steps from the subway and hoped she'd make it to her office building before the drizzle turned into a downpour, but as luck would have it, she didn't. She jogged to her building to get out of the rain as quickly as she could.

Once inside she was winded and soaking wet. She peered at the clock over the information desk, and she was over an hour late. She was grateful she didn't have a meeting, but not being on time for work wasn't professional, and being the only black woman in the office, she had to be ten times better than her coworkers, because they weren't comrades. They were opponents. That was it. She had to call Tracy.

After she got to her office, she headed straight to the ladies' room. She used the hand dryer to take some of the moisture from her blouse, and she dried her face with a paper towel. She slicked her hair down as best she could, and she reapplied her makeup so she could look presentable. As soon as she made it back to her office, she asked her assistant to get Stone Cold Towing on the line. By the time she made it to her desk, the call was on the line.

"Tracy Stone, please," she asked.

"Ma'am, I'm sorry, he's in the field today," the man on the other end said. "You can try to reach him on his cell phone."

"I don't have his card with me. Can you give me that number?" She reached for a pad and pen.

"Sure." He recited the number to her, and she wrote it down.

"Thank you, sir. Have a good day," she said and hung up. She then had second thoughts about calling. Was it the right thing to take an offer so great from a complete stranger? She questioned herself and then thought about her crazy morning, and dialed Tracy quickly, before she lost her nerve.

"Hi, this is Tracy." His voice was so deep and sexy to her.

She paused and almost forgot why she had called him. "Tracy, hi, this is Sha . . . I mean, November," she said nervously.

"Novey, how are you?"

Now he wanted to shorten her name, she thought, but she didn't address it. "Not too good."

"Why? What's going on?" He sounded concerned.

"No car is what is going on, and it is killing me. I need a car, and I wanted to know, does your offer still stand?"

"Of course."

"Thank you, thank you, thank you," she said, letting out a sigh of relief.

"No, it's no problem. I can get you the car today if you need me to."

"Can you? I'd really appreciate it. This bus thing is not working."

"I feel you on that. I've owned a car since I was sixteen. No way can I do CTA."

November leaned back in her chair. "I know that's right."

"So what time will you be free?" he asked.

"Whatever is convenient for you. I don't wanna interrupt your schedule."

"It doesn't matter to me. I don't have a set schedule."

"Well, I get off at four thirty today. I am leaving a little early so I can try to beat the work rush."

"Okay. Will six thirty be cool? I can come by and pick you up."

"That is fine. I should be home by then."

"Okay, great," he said.

"Tracy, I do appreciate this, and I owe you big time. If ever I can do anything for you in the future, please don't hesitate to ask."

"Oh, really? I will keep that in mind." His voice sounded seductive, and she wished she could take that statement back.

"Okay, Tracy, I guess I'll see you later."

"Okay."

They hung up. November felt so much better knowing that was her last day on the bus. She could have back those few extra moments of sleep in the morning she'd had to sacrifice.

She looked over a couple of accounts but couldn't stop thinking about Tracy. She wondered how many other helpless women he had done this for. How many women had he just hooked up with a car? Was he single or did he have a woman in his life?

He's fine as hell, and his body is so sexy. She wanted to know how good he tasted. She had wondered that ever since she'd seen him looking as good as he did the other night. And he was smooth and easy to talk to. She knew how Sagittarius women were, but this was her first experience with a male Sagittarius. He seemed outgoing like she was, and he did have his own business. *Can he be dateable?* she asked herself.

If he was dateable, would he even want to date her? He had come over and chilled with her for a minute, yes, but that didn't mean he would want her. Hell, he had waited until it was time to go before he finally flirted with her a little so, honestly, she didn't know what to think. She didn't have a lot of experience in the relationship department. She had had a couple boyfriends in the past, but nothing long-term, just a bunch of crap.

She had been living in and out of her parents' house during her college days, so that limited what she could and could not do. Having a relationship with a man while living with her parents was like trying to escape from Alcatraz. It was just not going to happen. When she did like a guy and thought it was cool to let him come over, her daddy preached to them about fornication. After, they'd be scared to touch her, like her daddy was God and could see them sucking on her nipples in the dark. Her experiences with the guys she did date were short. She had never even been in love before. Nothing had lasted long enough.

All she focused on lately was moving into her new condo and her career in advertising. Love had been the last thing on her mind, but she found herself thinking of putting it on her "things to do" list. She wondered if she should ask Tracy out or just leave it alone. Hell, she didn't know. When it came to men and relationships, she was stumped.

Shaking her head, she put him out of her thoughts and thanked God that she would no longer be riding the bus.

Chapter Four

"Hey, come on in," she told Tracy, inviting him into her apartment. "I'll be ready in a moment." She walked toward her bedroom to change. She still had on her work clothes because she had just walked in about five minutes before he got there. "Have a seat," she yelled over her shoulder.

She went into her room and found something cute to put on. She fingered through her short bob, which was finally dry from the morning rain, and she ran her Clinique sponge over her face to take away the shine. Then she applied a fresh coat of gloss to her lips. She changed her jewelry to more casual pieces and slipped on her light leather jacket and grabbed her purse. She did a quick squirt of cotton blossom and did her last mirror check before rejoining Tracy in the living room.

He was still standing when she came back, and she wondered if he had heard her offer him a seat. "Hey, thanks for waiting. You could have taken a seat."

"Naw. I got on these dirty clothes, and I didn't wanna sit on your light-colored furniture."

"Oh, thanks, but don't worry. That sofa is not going to my new place. God willing, I plan to have new furniture when I move."

"Oh, I see. But still . . ." He looked down at his uniform.

"No problem. Are you ready?"

"Yeah, let's go," he said.

They walked out to his SUV with every eye in the building on them. Her nosy neighbors never missed a thing, because most of them were always perched in their windows peering out at all the things that went on in their courtyard.

Ms. Wanda, being the boldest of them all, spoke up. "Good evening, young man. You taking my Shareese out for the evening?"

"My Shareese." She ain't my damn momma, November said to herself. "Ms. Wanda, leave folks alone and mind your business. Don't worry about where I'm going."

"Chile, somebody ought to know in case old Boris Kodjoe here tries something. Just because he fine don't make him sane." Ms. Wanda popped her gum and took a puff of her Newport.

"And neither does he concern you. Good night," November said. She and Tracy hurried to his truck and rode out.

By the time they made it to the car lot, it was dark. "Are they closed?" November asked suspiciously. She was a little scared, and she wondered if he was into some illegal mess.

He pulled up in front. "Yeah, but I have the keys," he said.

They got out, and he put his key inside of the glass door to unlock it. November looked around, praying that the feds and helicopters wouldn't come out of nowhere and take her to jail.

Tracy opened one of the glass doors and let her go in before him. Inside, November could hear a man's voice from the lit-up office a few feet away from where she was standing. She hadn't thought anyone was there. She had never been in a car dealership after business hours, and she felt like something may be a little fishy with what they were doing, but she didn't ask any questions.

"Trey, is that you, man?" the voice yelled from the office.

"Yeah, it's me!" he yelled back at him as he locked the front door.

"I'll be out in a second. I called Shawn to pull the truck around before he left," the voice said.

November walked over and looked in the window of a Maxima that was on the showroom floor. She was careful not to touch the glass because she didn't want her prints on anything. She noticed cameras in the ceiling, so she went to sit on the leather sofa. If they had her on tape, there would not be much to pin on her if she was just sitting, she thought.

After a couple moments, a handsome, older version of Tracy came from the office. They were definitely brothers. November laughed on the inside because she didn't think he looked like a typical car salesman. He wasn't what she expected when she had heard his voice coming from the office.

She gave him a once-over. He was dapper, clean-cut with a nicely trimmed beard and mustache, and he had what looked like an amazing body under the expensive-looking suit that fit him to perfection. He and Tracy were almost the same height, but Tracy may have been slightly taller.

"Hey, li'l brother, what's up?"

"Nothing too much, man. How are things around here?" Tracy asked, looking around the room.

"Good, man, things are good. You must be November," he said, extending a hand to her.

"Yes, I am," she said, standing and shaking his hand.

"Nice to meet you. So, Trey tells me that you need some wheels until you close on your new place?"

"Yes, sir, that is correct."

"Okay, but please call me Trent. I'm only three years older than Tracy, and 'sir' is not the way you address a young man." He laughed.

"Well, that means you are right, since that makes you two years older than me." She looked at Tracy, bragging that she was older.

"Yes, Tracy did mention that your birthday was on the same day as his."

"Yeah, that shocked me too," November said.

"Well, come on out and let's see if you like the vehicle he picked out for you."

She looked over at Tracy. She was sure that Trent was not supposed to say "the one he picked out for you." When they got outside, she followed Trent apprehensively. She was still a bit uneasy, but she did her best not to let it show. They stopped at a Denali.

"Do you like it?" Trent asked, handing her the keys.

"You're joking, right?"

"No. Open the door and get in and tell me if this will be okay."

"I don't have to get in. This is more than okay. I mean, I expected a Dodge Neon or a Hyundai or something, but this is a Denali," she said, shaking her head.

"Do you like?" Tracy asked, walking up behind her.

"Tracy, thank you, but I can't take this." She tried to hand him the keys.

"Why not?"

"'Cause I can't. Trent, do you have something else? I mean, something less expensive, like a Corolla or a Sentra or a Yugo? I will take a Yugo, I swear."

The men burst into laughter.

"So this means you like it?" Tracy asked again.

"Yes, I like it. Who wouldn't like a pretty, shiny black Denali with rims and gold accents?" She touched the door. "But, Tracy, this is a bit much, don't you think?"

"Why don't you get in and take it out for a spin and then tell me if you want something else?" Tracy said.

Trent backed up. "Yes, that is a good idea. Take it and test it out. I betcha then you will love it." Now he sounded like a car salesman, November thought.

She hesitated for a moment then agreed. Even if she wouldn't keep it, she could take the opportunity to drive it. She and Tracy got in, and Trent went back inside.

They pulled out, and November was excited. The truck was fully loaded. She stopped at a light and could see the reflection of the Denali on a mirrored building. She liked the way it looked.

The longer she drove, the more she relaxed and enjoyed the smooth, comfortable ride. It was spacious, and she knew she wasn't driving an Accord.

"So you think you can live with this for a few weeks?" Tracy asked when he saw her smiling.

"Hell, I could live with this for a few years," she said. They laughed.

"Well, when you close on your place, you can always purchase it."

"Man, are you crazy? This is not in my budget, especially after I get my new mortgage."

"Don't worry about all of that. I'm sure my brother will give you an excellent deal."

"Oh, yeah?" she said, thinking that maybe then she could.

"Yeah. We can see about you getting the family discount." He smiled.

By the time they got back to the dealership, Trent was getting into his Mercedes to leave. When he saw them pull in, he put his briefcase on the seat and went over to them.

"So you like it?" he asked.

November smiled. "Yes, I like it."

"Well, good. Y'all have a good night. I gotta get home to the fam." He walked away, and Tracy and November sat in the truck for a few moments.

"Tracy, this is very generous of you and Trent. I have to give you something for allowing me to use this truck. I will write you a check."

"That won't be necessary, November. All the paperwork is right here in the glove box, and if you have any problems with it, let me know and I'll take care of it."

"Please, Tracy. I really appreciate this, and I wouldn't feel right not giving you something."

"Listen, I am only helping a person I am in a position to help. Your thank-you is enough."

"Okay, I understand, and I do thank you for helping me out. This is above and beyond the help I thought I'd receive. I will take care of your Denali, and I will do my very best to get it back to you in the condition that it's in," she said. God was finally cutting her some slack. After all the pain and anguish she had been going through, losing her car and the horrible accident she was in, things were taking a turn for the better.

"I'm sure you will. Now, do you know your way back from here?"

"No, not really. I have never driven out this way before."

"Well, follow me and I'll get you to the expressway. Unless you wanna use the fancy navigation system that is in here."

She gave him a warm smile. "No, I prefer to follow you."

"Okay." He smiled back at her.

He closed the door, and she squeezed the steering wheel. She smiled and looked over her shoulder to see if Tracy had gotten into his truck. He pulled up to the side of her and got out and handed her her purse. She had forgotten that she'd left it on the front seat floor when they went inside.

"Oh, shit. Thank you, Tracy. I forgot all about my purse."

"No problem. Just follow me," he said and got back into his truck.

She rode behind him until they reached her exit and she flashed her lights to let him know she was getting off. She wished he were coming back to her place, but since he didn't ask, she didn't offer. When she got home, she got lucky and found an open parking space right in front of her building.

As she approached the building, she saw Roderick looking down at her. "Hey, November," he said like he had always called her that name.

"Roderick, I ain't in the mood," she said with attitude.

"Nice set of wheels there, Miss Shareese. Wanna take an old man for a ride?"

"In your dreams," she said and entered the building. On her way down the hall, she heard his door unlock, so she tried to hurry past his unit.

"Umm, who wheels you pushin'? That drug dealer we saw you leave with?" He moved to stand in front of her and lowered his voice. "You know I need me a few trees for my glaucoma."

"Move outta my way, Roderick, and mind your business. How many times must I tell y'all that? Y'all don't need to know everything about what I do, and no, Tracy ain't no dealer. And you know ain't nothing wrong with yo' eyes, old man. Now move so I can go upstairs."

"It is too something wrong with my eyes. You've known that since you've been here. I have glaucoma. And you know don't nothing go on in this building that we don't know about, so don't be acting like you all that, Miss Thang. And where you get the money for that pretty truck if he ain't no drug dealer?"

"Good night, Roderick," she said, moving past him. "And since you are the neighborhood watch, go back to your post and make sure nothing happens to my truck."

"Okay, but you know I am gonna need a little something for keeping an eye on your nice truck."

"Thank you," she said and went into her apartment. She knew he would watch her truck all night if he had to, because he wanted to know and see it all. One thing she did like about her snooping neighbors was that they kept the place from being broken into, and nobody's car was stolen because somebody, somewhere in that building was watching and making sure they didn't miss a thing.

Chapter Five

By Saturday, she hadn't heard from Tracy, so she decided she'd call him as soon as she got in from shopping. After fighting traffic and climbing the steps with a few bags of goodies for her new place, she was tired. She hit the play button on her iPod and went to shower and wash her hair. At about eight o'clock she called him. She got his voice mail. She left him a brief message and threw on some sweats and a T-shirt. She was looking through her new things when her cell phone vibrated on the coffee table.

She looked at the ID and was pleased to see that it was Tracy returning her call. "Hey, Tracy, how are you?"

"I am fine, and how are you?"

"Good. I'm doing well."

"How is the truck working for you?"

"Aww, man, it's nice. I am definitely enjoying it."

"That's good to hear. So what's up with you? What are you getting into tonight?"

"Nothing, just gon' hang around the house."

"Nonsense. You wanna hang out with me?"

"What are you getting into?"

"Well, a friend of mine is having a birthday bash tonight at Spot 6. Do you wanna go?"

"Sure. What time should I meet you there?"

"Oh, so since you got wheels, a brother can't pick you up?"

"No, nothing like that. I just didn't think that you'd wanna come and get me. But if you do, that's cool with me. I just didn't want to assume anything. You could have been picking up your woman or something, you know." She hoped that wasn't the case.

"Well, I told you before that I am a single man. And if I were bringing a woman, no way I'd invite another woman to come hang out with me."

"Oh, okay. You just never know nowadays."

"Well, I try to make it a point not to lie to people, because that leads to more lies, and I don't even want to go there with anyone, especially you."

"Oh, especially me? Why is that?"

"Because you seem too sincere. I don't have any reason to bullshit you."

She frowned. "So you're admitting that you bullshit women?"

"Honestly, there are women I've lied to, but it was usually to keep from hurting their feelings, or I knew that they were on some old bullshit, so I bullshit back with them."

"Oh, okay. I see how you operate."

"No, don't take it like that. There are women you meet, and you go out with them once or twice, and you learn early that they are not the one you wanna continue to kick it with. Some are nice, so you can't just say, 'Hey, you suck, and I don't want to go out with you anymore.' You have to tell them something that will not hurt them, and usually it's a lie. Because if it ain't truth, I don't care how you try to justify it, it is a lie. When I say I have lied to women before, it's because I don't like to see people hurt."

"Since you put it that way, I've lied to men too."

"See? You know how it can be."

"Yeah, I do," she said. Her frown vanished. She was relieved at his answer. It made sense. People normally don't just tell a person to get lost; they make up some lame excuse to keep from being the bad guy.

"So, are you gon' kick it with me tonight or what?"

"Sure. What time should I be ready?"

"Ten will be cool."

"I can be ready by ten. That's fine."

"All right, then. I will see you then."

She hung up and went to her bedroom. She had to find something to wear quickly if she was going to be ready on time. Going through her closet, she was mad that she had put on a few pounds and a lot of her jeans were super tight. She spent almost forty-five minutes just finding something cute to wear. She was happy that she had shampooed and wrapped her hair when she got in, because she didn't have to spend a lot of time styling it.

By nine thirty, she was putting on makeup. She was picking out jewelry when her cell phone rang. It was Tracy telling her he was downstairs parking and he would be right up. She hurried and put on her earrings and necklace, but she couldn't get her bracelet on. She put it on the table and decided she'd ask Tracy to help her. She was checking her face one more time when he knocked on the door.

When she opened the door, her jaw almost dropped to the floor. Tracy was looking damn good. Mr. Stone was definitely looking Stone cold.

"Come on in. I just have to get my purse," she said, walking away.

She wondered how it was possible for him to keep getting finer by the day. She grabbed her purse and turned off her bedroom light. When she went back into the living room, he was still standing near the door.

"You look nice," she said.

"So do you." His eyes were on her, and she could tell he was checking out her curves in her jeans. She bent over to get her bracelet from the coffee table, and she heard him make a little hissing sound.

She looked at him and tilted her head. "Did you just hiss at me?"

"My bad. I . . . I didn't mean for that to come out."

She let him off the hook. She was glad that he noticed her because she had tried to look her best for him, even though she knew it wasn't a date.

"Here, can you put this on for me?" she asked, handing him her bracelet. He smiled and put it on for her.

"Are we all set?" he asked.

"Yeah. Do you think I need a jacket?"

"It's pretty nice, but later it may be a little chilly," he said.

She opened her coat closet and grabbed a light leather jacket. They walked out, and he waited for her to lock her door. She was nervous, and she didn't know why.

When they got to the party, she tried to stay close to Tracy since she didn't know anyone, but somehow, they kept getting separated. People were pulling him in every direction, and she was a little jealous when she saw women talking to him.

"Are you having a good time?" Jonathan, one of Tracy's friends, asked her when he noticed her standing alone. Tracy had introduced them when they first got to the party.

"Yes, everything is nice. I'm having a good time."

"That's good. It's November, right?"

"Yes, it is," she said, wishing that Tracy would call her Shareese like everybody else she knew called her.

"So, are you enjoying yourself?" he asked again. November assumed he was nervous or just trying to make conversation with her.

"Yes, I am." Jonathan was cute, but she had her eyes on Tracy. She sipped her wine and hoped he would get back to her again.

"So, how long have you and Trey been together?" he asked.

That caught her off guard. She and Tracy were not a couple, nor were they together. "Tracy and I aren't together. We are friends."

"Oh, is that right?" He moved closer to her, so close he was in her face. It made her uncomfortable.

She took a step back. "Yes, that's right, we are just friends."

"Well then, November, would you like to dance?"

She had no clue where Tracy had sneaked off to, and the music was jamming, so she agreed. They danced for a couple of songs, and she was enjoying herself until she spotted Tracy talking to a woman who was absolutely gorgeous. She had a bad-ass body, and her brown complexion looked flawless.

November couldn't take her eyes off Tracy talking and smiling with the beautiful woman. She wanted to go over and interrupt, but she couldn't bring herself to leave the dance floor because the music was jamming and she didn't want to let him ruin her good time. The song changed to Ne-Yo's "Sexy Love, " and she went back to dancing with Jonathan. That was one of her favorite songs, and she hadn't heard it in a long while. She had burned a hole in that track years ago when she bought the CD.

She saw Tracy watching her dance with Jonathan. She smiled, but he barely smiled back. When the song went off, she headed to the bathroom to dab the sweat from her face and refresh her makeup. She walked past Tracy and the woman without stopping. She didn't feel it was necessary to interrupt, but she wanted Tracy to know she saw him chatting with her.

When she was done freshening up, she went back to the party. Tracy was no longer standing where he had been, so she looked around for him.

"Hey, November," Jonathan said, coming up behind her.

"Jonathan, hey," she said dryly.

"Wanna get back out there?" he asked, pointing to the floor.

"No, I need a drink. I have to cool off a bit."

"Hold on, I'll get one for you." He dashed to the bar.

He hadn't even asked her what she wanted, but she didn't care. She was just glad he was gone for a second so she could look for Tracy. When she spotted him, she was about to walk over to him, but Jonathan came back with a glass of white wine. He must have seen what she was drinking earlier. He was sweet, cute, and attentive, but she still had her mind on Tracy. She didn't want to let the gorgeous woman he was talking to intimidate her, but for some reason, she did.

"Thanks, Jonathan," she said and took a sip. "Listen, I need to step outside to get some air real quick. Can you hold this for me?" She handed him her glass.

"Sure thing. I'll be right here when you get back."

"I bet," she said with sarcasm and a smile.

She walked outside and took a couple of deep breaths and let the night air cool her off. She went back in and saw Tracy talking to another woman. *Just forget it,* she told herself. It was apparent he wasn't interested in her, so she went back over to Jonathan. At least he was entertaining her.

"Hey, Jonathan, thanks for holding my drink," she said.

He handed it to her. "No problem. Do you feel better now?"

"Yeah, just needed to get a little air. You know a sista ain't trying to sweat her hair out," she said, fanning herself.

"Yeah, I know, right," he said.

They continued talking for a few moments and November saw Tracy heading in their direction.

"Hey, you," he said, interrupting them. "I want to know what Jonathan is saying to make you smile so brightly."

"What's up, man. I see you're having a good time," Jonathan said.

"Yeah, I see you are having one too. Keeping my girl company?"

Jonathan looked confused. November was in the same state of confusion. He sounded almost . . . jealous? But that couldn't be the case. She had observed him talking to several other women, fine women at that.

"Yeah, you can say that," Jonathan snapped back, "since you left her all alone."

"No, just giving her some space to enjoy the party."

"Yeah, all right, man," Jonathan said. "November, it was nice talking to you. Enjoy the party." He walked away.

"What was that?" she asked Tracy.

"What was what?" he asked.

"That."

"I don't know what you're talking about." He gave her an innocent look, and she smiled on the inside. It was nice for him to show a little interest.

"The 'my girl' business?" she said and sipped her wine.

"I didn't mean it like that. I just meant my homegirl. And I'm ready to head out. Are you ready to go?"

"Yeah, if you are," she said and drank the rest of her drink.

"Okay, let's get outta here."

"All right." She followed him out the door.

"I'll get the truck. You wait right here," he said and went to the parking lot.

While she waited for him to pull around, two women from the party came out looking for Tracy, and she overheard them talking.

"Where is he? He just walked out," one said.

"I know. I guess I missed him, and I didn't even get his number."

"Girl, you'll see Tracy again. And if I were you, I'd let it go, because every time he sees you, he plays you."

"He does not. He's just playing hard to get."

"That's because he ain't trying to get got."

"That's what his mouth says, but one day I'm gon' get his ass."

Tracy finally pulled up. When he stopped, the girl thought he was stopping for her. When November approached the door, she was embarrassed.

"Damn, it's like that?" she said.

"I told you to let it go," her friend said and walked off.

November closed her door and smiled a little to see that she wasn't the only one checking Tracy. She felt good when he picked her up, even though nothing was going on.

They drove back to her place in silence. November dozed off on the way, and when he parked, he tapped her thigh to wake her.

"Wake up, sleepyhead, we're here."

"Aww, already?" she said, sitting up. She didn't want to climb the steps to her place.

"Yes, already, sleepyhead. I thought you would keep me company, but you were slobbering as soon as we got on the highway."

"I'm sorry. It's the wine, I guess."

"It's all good. Can I walk you up?"

"Sure," she said and undid her seat belt. She grabbed her jacket and put it on before she got out. When they got on her floor, she opened the door and walked in.

Tracy stood in the hall. "Well, good night, November. I hope you had a good time."

"I did. You're not gonna come in for a minute?" she asked, standing in front of the door. He looked good as hell.

"I don't think I should." He seemed nervous, rubbing his hands together.

"Why? Do you have to get home and feed your dog or something?" she asked, making a joke.

"No." He laughed.

"Well then, come in," she offered again. He didn't budge. "Well, suit yourself. Good night, Tra—"

He silenced her when he pulled her into his arms and kissed her passionately. He kissed her better and sweeter than she could remember ever being kissed before. It sent waves all over her body. She wanted him.

He touched her, running his hands over her body and squeezing her ass. Her nipples were awakened, and her juices started to flow.

"Tracy. Tracy," she whispered between kisses. "What are we doing?"

He released her and backed up. "I'm sorry."

She hated that she'd said something. She hadn't wanted him to stop.

"Look, November, I didn't mean to do that. I apologize," he said.

She put a hand up to stop him. "Tracy, you don't have to apologize, and I don't want you to leave." She smiled.

"Are you sure, November? Are you sure you want me to stay?"

"Yes." She moved closer to him, intending to show him that she was interested.

He kissed her again, pushing her back inside, and she kicked the door closed with her foot. She pulled away long enough to lock the door, and they went into her bedroom. As soon as they crossed the threshold of her bedroom, they got into back-breaking, hold-your-breath, oh-my-God type of sex.

When they were done, she didn't think about the next morning or what they were doing or going to be. She just drifted into a peaceful sleep in his arms. She woke up a couple hours later to go to the bathroom, and before she could go back to sleep, he wanted more. She gave it to him.

He went deep inside of her again, making her bed rock and leaving November under a Stone-cold spell.

Chapter Six

The ringing phone jerked November out of her sleep. She was exhausted from the glorious sex that she and Tracy had the night before and that morning. It was after two in the afternoon, and they were unable to pull themselves out of bed. She was lying so close to his warm, naked body that they were stuck together from their sweat.

She managed to inch away from his body to get the ringing phone from the cradle. "Hello," she answered in a sleepy voice.

"November Shareese McKinney, why were you not in church this morning?" The voice echoed through the phone like she was a six-year-old.

"Daddy?" she asked, surprised.

"Yes, young lady. You know today was the appreciation service for your mother, and you weren't there."

She sat up. "Oh, Daddy, I'm so sorry," she said, rubbing her head. How could she have forgotten the ceremony? Her momma had reminded her almost every day, and she had still forgotten.

"Yes, you should be. Your mother was so upset to not see you."

"I'm so sorry, Daddy. I wasn't feeling well last night, and I guess the medicine I took had me out. I would have never missed Mom's ceremony, it's just I think I'm coming down with a virus or something." She gave a fake cough. "And I took some meds and drank Theraflu," she said, still lying.

That was the best she could come up with. She couldn't say it was getting her ass waxed by an incredibly fine-ass man named Tracy that put her out. She couldn't tell her daddy she woke up with a dick inside of her and that was why she didn't go to church.

"Yeah, okay, pumpkin. But you should have called your momma last night. That way, she wouldn't have been so disappointed."

"I know, Daddy, I just didn't know I would miss it. I had my alarm set and everything." She had to hurry and get off the phone because she hated lying to her parents.

She felt Tracy bump her and she put a finger to her lips so he would keep quiet. If her daddy knew she missed her momma's event due to lying up with some guy, he'd never let her off the phone.

"Well, your mother will be all right, just be sure to call her this evening."

"Where is she?"

"She's still at the church. They've got a program for the teenagers today, and you know your daddy can't tolerate them youngsters."

"I know, Daddy." She laughed. Her daddy was the oldest of the old-fashioned.

"Well, pumpkin, I hope you feel better soon."

"Okay, Daddy. I'll call Ma later on this evening," she said, glad to be getting off the phone.

"Okay, darling, feel better," he said.

"Okay. Bye now." She did another fake cough before she hung up.

"Oh, so you got a virus?" Tracy asked, teasing.

"Be quiet, man. It's because of you I missed an important ceremony for my mother today."

"Oh, now you gon' blame me? As I recall, you were the one in the hall last night all on a brother, not wanting me to leave."

"Man, please," she said, smiling.

"And it was you saying, 'Ooh, Tracy, baby. Right there. Yeah, baby. Yes, baby. Ooh, ooh.'"

She hit him with her pillow, and he laughed. She smiled, and he began to caress her back. His touch was so nice. She closed her eyes and sighed.

"November," he said softly.

"Yes?"

"What happened between us was good, and I'd like to get to know you a little better. I'm not looking to rush into anything."

That made her a little uneasy. Men never want to rush into anything, but they rush the panties. They always want to tap that ass.

"Well, Tracy, to be honest, I don't want to rush either, so there is no pressure. I didn't expect this to happen, but I'm not naming our children or nothing like that." She smiled, hoping he understood that she knew sleeping together didn't make them a couple.

"Okay. I just don't want you to think that I'm trying to play you, because I'm not. I have been in a couple of relationships, and people were hurt. I don't wanna hurt you, nor do I wanna get hurt. You are a beautiful woman, and I do like you, but I just want us to take it slow."

"That's fine. I don't have any problem with that."

"Cool. So, are you hungry? Because a brotha is starving."

"Man, yes."

He spoke between soft kisses on her neck. "How about we get dressed, go grab a bite, and then come back and do what we did this morning?"

"How about no?" she returned.

"Huh?"

"How you gon' give me the 'let's take it slow' speech and try to get me sprung at the same time?" His dick was too good. She'd be a stalker with him messing with her like that.

"Oh, so you don't wanna do it again?"

"No, I didn't say that, but if we are taking things slow, I'm not trying to get set up. The shit is good, and I will not become a Tracy addict."

He got up. "Okay then, I gotcha." His body was killer, she thought as he stretched. "Let's shower and go eat, and then we go from there."

"Sounds good," she said.

Not five minutes later, they were in the shower together.

It was going to be so hard to not fall for him and not want him, November thought as he sucked her nipples. He had a way with her body that she had never experienced before.

They finally managed to get out of her apartment by dinnertime. They ate and talked and laughed. November had a good time with him. He was so cool, and there was no denying that they were feeling each other. She secretly hoped he would become her man.

They went back to her apartment and relaxed on the couch and watched a couple movies.

It was close to eleven when she realized she hadn't called her mom. She knew that would have to be the first thing done the next morning.

The twelve o'clock hour was approaching fast, and she started to get sad. Tracy would be leaving soon. They both had to work the next day, and she should have been heading to bed because she was not a morning person. She fought the urge to yawn, but couldn't help herself.

"You tired?" Tracy asked.

"Yeah, a little," she responded, hoping he wouldn't take that as a sign to go.

"Well, it's late. I should be going." He got up from the sofa.

"Yeah. I'm going to shower and lay it down."

"Can I call you when I get in?" he asked.

Aww, now he wanna call a sista, she thought, smiling inside. "Sure, you can call me if you wanna call." Somehow, she couldn't stop smiling around him.

"Yeah, just to say good night."

She walked him to the door. "Okay then, call me to say good night, if you'd like."

They stood there for a few moments, kissing slow and sweet.

"Good night, Tracy," November said, breaking their embrace.

"Good night, November. I'll call you when I make it home."

"Okay."

She stepped into the hall and watched him walk down the steps. When the downstairs door closed, she heard Roderick open his door.

"Aww snap, Shareese, you finally getting some," he said, teasing her like he was a ten-year-old.

"Roderick," she yelled in annoyance.

"I know, I know. Mind my business."

"Exactly!"

"I would, but keep in mind you can hear through these vents, girlfriend. And what I heard last night and this morning and this afternoon made your business my business."

"Well, if you hear my business again, act like you don't. Good night, Roderick!" She slammed her door. "Damn, I can't wait to get outta this building. These are the nosiest folks in the world. Damn!" she yelled and went to take her shower.

Chapter Seven

That night, Tracy called November, and they ended up staying on the phone until after two a.m. She was tired the next day at work and couldn't wait to get home and lie down. He called her, wanting to come over, but she was too tired. Although she wanted to see him, she couldn't open her eyes long enough to even talk to him on the phone. She didn't want to say no, but she did. Their schedules were tight the next couple of days, so they didn't see each other, just traded lots of phone calls and text messages.

Thursday, she told herself to wait one more night to see him so she wouldn't have to get up the next morning, but it was impossible for them to stay away from each other another evening. After Tracy promised that he wouldn't keep her up late, she agreed to let him come over. She made it home by six thirty, and he was at her place fifteen minutes later.

When he got upstairs, they kissed for an eter-
nity, it seemed, to make up for the days they
hadn't seen one another. She reminded herself
not to allow this fine-ass man to reel her in, but
his kisses were so intoxicating. She knew if she
didn't watch it, she'd be in love. She backed
away from the kiss and let out a breath to calm
herself. If they kept it up, she would be naked
in her living room, which wasn't a bad idea, but
they had plans to go out to dinner.

"Come on, Tracy, we betta cut this out before
something happens."

"Well, in that case, let's not stop," he said,
grabbing her and giving her another kiss.

"Come on, baby, stop it. I'm hungry. You said
you'd take me to dinner and let me get some rest
tonight."

"Okay, okay. I'll leave you alone. For now." He
grinned a devilish grin.

She put on her shoes and got her purse so
they could leave. They went to a nice restaurant
downtown where they ate good food and enjoyed
wine and the nice atmosphere.

She excused herself to go to the ladies' room,
and when she got back, she saw a woman walking away from their table. What was going on?
November watched her smile over her shoulder
at Tracy. And he was smiling back.

When she sat down, she didn't say a word or ask him any questions. She played with her food, barely eating it, because that woman had made her feel so uneasy. Did they exchange numbers? Did Tracy even tell her that he was on a date? Why did she walk away giving him a seductive glance over her shoulder? Tracy acted as if nothing happened and he kept the conversation going during dinner, even though she was short with her responses and didn't add much commentary to the conversations they exchanged.

When they got in the truck to ride back to her place, she had a little attitude, but she didn't say anything. After all, he wasn't her man.

"Are you okay?" he asked.

"I'm fine," she said sharply.

"No, you're not. What's wrong?"

"It's nothing, Tracy. Don't worry about it."

"Okay," he said.

Being the sensitive Sagittarius she was, she got even angrier. She knew it was childish, but she wanted him to figure it out or at least try harder to see what was bothering her, but he didn't. When they got back to her place, she hopped out before he had the opportunity to get the door for her. She walked ahead of him, and when she got inside, she threw her keys on the table.

"Okay, November," Tracy said, "I'm not a mind reader, and I can't fix it if you don't tell me what's bothering you." He sounded genuinely concerned.

Now, she was too embarrassed to say what it was. "Listen, Tracy, I'm just bugging out, okay? I'm cool."

"You sure?" He lifted her chin and looked her in the eyes.

"Yes," she said with a faint smile.

He smiled at her. "Okay then, give me a better smile than that one."

She tried to look like she was fine, but she could tell he knew that she wasn't completely cool. She stood there for a moment or two with her fake smile then she turned away to remove her shoes. She excused herself to her bedroom and was about to peel off her clothes when she heard music from her living room. When she went back out, Tracy wasn't in the living room. He came out of the kitchen and handed her a glass of wine. She took it and smiled, deciding to drop the attitude.

He pulled her into his arms. "Novey, just relax. This could be good if you just chill and take it one day at a time and we take our time to get to know each other. Don't get upset over small things, baby. I know that scene at the restaurant with the chick walking by the table brought on the attitude, but I'm not that guy. She spoke, asked if I was dining alone, and I told her I wasn't. She flirted a little and said that was too bad, and she continued on her way. It was nothing, and nothing happened. If we make it, it will just be you and me. I don't share with others, so just relax and let's just see how it goes."

The tension eased in her shoulders. She smiled and relaxed as they swayed to the music. After a couple of sips of her merlot and a slow dance, they made their way into her bedroom.

They were into making each other feel good when she remembered she needed to keep her voice down. Nosy-ass Roderick probably had his ear to the vent. She had a hard time being quiet, and her soft moans and heavy breathing echoed off the empty walls of her room. She had taken everything off, getting ready for her move. Her body sang as he stroked her insides with his instrument.

They went two wonderful rounds before they finally passed out. Before she knew it, her alarm buzzed. She couldn't believe that the morning had already come. She dragged herself to the shower trying not to wake Tracy, but she failed.

He stepped into the shower with her, and she pleaded with him to allow her to shower and get to work on time. She was tired. He had her drained from the previous night. Her pussy was sore, and all she wanted to do was shower, grab a cup of coffee, and make it through another long day.

"So what time do you have to be at work?" she asked him as she poured him a cup of coffee in her extra thermos.

"Whenever I get there," he responded.

She handed him the cup. "Oh, I forgot you're the boss man," she said, teasing.

"Yep, that's what they call me." He smiled and sipped his hot coffee.

"Well, I gotta get out of here," she said, pouring her coffee into her Starbucks thermos cup, "because, not like you, I have to be there at eight thirty."

"You want me to take you?" he asked.

"You wanna take me to work?" she asked, surprised.

"Yeah, I can take you, and I'll pick you up this evening."

She thought it was an awesome idea. She hated driving to work in the traffic. "Okay, that'll work, but please don't be late picking me up, because Lord knows I am tired today and I want to get home as soon as I can."

"I won't be late, trust me. And why are you so tired?"

She raised an eyebrow. "You have to ask me that, Mr. All Night Long?"

"Oh, yeah, sorry. Sometimes I get a little, you know, carried away. Especially when it's good." He grabbed her from behind and kissed her neck. "Why don't you take the day off?"

"No, Tracy, I can't," she said, breaking away.

"Why not? Call in sick or something," he suggested.

"I told you I was saving my days for my move."

"I know, but it's only one day. Come on, we can hang out all day and . . . you know." He nodded toward the bedroom.

"Nice try, but I can't. I have to save my days. Trust me, as tired as I am, I would love to not go in, but I can't."

"All right, I understand that. But if you can get off early, let me know."

November smiled to herself. She could tell he was digging her. She got her things, and they headed out the door. When he dropped her off, he told her that he may not be able to get her for lunch and she told him it was cool because she usually had lunch with one of her coworkers. They kissed, and he promised he'd be right there at six.

She went up to her floor and couldn't concentrate on work. All she could think about was Tracy. She contemplated whether she should take a half day, but she ended up staying the entire day because she had a couple of afternoon meetings that she couldn't reschedule last minute. In her last meeting, she almost had a panic attack, because the meeting had run over and she didn't want to be late meeting Tracy that evening.

As soon as the meeting was adjourned, she made a mad dash to her office and quickly gathered her things. She almost knocked her assistant over when she jetted out of her office. "I'm so sorry," she said in a rush but kept moving. When she finally got downstairs and walked out the revolving doors, he was there just like he said he would be, waiting for her.

She climbed in and apologized for being a few moments late, and they kissed and went to dinner. They spent the entire weekend together. November was on cloud nine.

Chapter Eight

Closing day arrived after a two-week delay. November was so ecstatic she couldn't sit still in the chair. Tracy had to remind her to bring it down a couple of times because she was bursting and her pitch was louder than normal when she conversed with the banking agent. After what felt like hours of signing papers, she finally had her keys in her hand, and she couldn't wait to leave the bank.

Unable to wait, she and Tracy headed over to her new place first before going to load up her things. Tracy had helped her by getting a few of his employees to help move her stuff. They were on their way back to her old apartment to start moving, and she was so excited she couldn't keep still.

"You're excited, I see," he said.

"Yes, of course I'm excited."

"And you should be. Your condo is very nice."

"Thank you. I can't wait to get all settled in."
She beamed as they headed to her place to load
up her truck.

When they got to her old place, Tracy insisted
she get out of the way while he and his crew han-
dled everything. She didn't argue, and she took
a few moments to go and say farewell to some of
her neighbors she loved, and to some, she was
glad to be getting away from. Ms. Wanda hugged
her so tight and long and carried on like her
only daughter was going away. November would
miss her old crazy-ass, nosy neighbors.

The guys got there and loaded her things
fairly quickly and unloaded just as fast. In six
hours she was completely moved in, and she was
tired. She just wanted to eat and close her eyes.
Her new furniture would be arriving the next
day, so she had to move boxes out of the way to
free up space.

She looked around and admired her new place.
This was the way she was supposed to be living,
not in that old, run-down apartment. Everything
was new and upgraded, and her hardwood floors
were gorgeous. She couldn't wait to get orga-
nized. She walked over and touched the exposed
brick on the wall. It looked even better than she
remembered. Her kitchen was spacious, and the
granite countertops and top-notch appliances

screamed for her to cook a meal. She rubbed her hands across the mahogany cabinetry. It was definitely a dream come true.

"So, are you ready?"

"Ready for what?" she asked Tracy.

"To go over to my place."

"No, man, that's okay. I'm good. I'm just hungry."

"Well, we can get a bite and then we can head to my place since you don't have a bed."

Although that made perfect sense, she wanted to spend her first night in her own place. "That sounds good, but you know I have to get up early and get some things done. I should stay here."

"Like what, Novey? There is no bed, and I can have you back here as early as you need to be."

"Are you sure?" she said, now agreeing with him. As much as she wanted to stay in her new place, she didn't want to sleep on the hard floor.

"Of course I'm sure," he said.

"Tracy, why are you so good to me?"

"Because . . ." He paused. "I've never met a woman like you, and if we make it, I promise I'll always be good to you."

She wondered why he always said, "if we make it." Why would they not make it? Hell, how would he know if they had made it?

She smiled and convinced him to go and get them something to eat. It was still early, and she wanted to do a little more before she left her place for the night. A few moments after he had gone, there was a knock at the door. *Who could that be?* she wondered as she moved toward the door. She had just moved in, and she couldn't think of anyone who'd be coming by.

She looked through the peephole. It was a guy. She opened the door a little to find out what he wanted, and she almost drooled. The brother was *fine*. Tyrese/Tyson Beckford–type fine, she thought when she got a good look at him.

"How can I help you?" she asked, trying not to smile.

"Hi, I'm Jerome. I live across the hall, and I just wanted to come over to introduce myself and welcome you to the building." He extended a hand. He looked over her shoulder as if he was trying to see into her place.

"Oh, hi, Jerome. I'm Shareese. Nice to meet you," she said, shaking his hand.

"Well, I don't mean to be rude, but I've been dying to see what this unit looks like on the inside. I moved in about three months ago when your unit was still under reno, and I've been dying to see what they did to the space. I'm a contractor myself, and I just opened my own business. Things are moving a little slow, so I would like to see what's hot."

"Sure, you can see, but I'm sure they are all standard," she said, opening the door.

"Not so," he said, coming in and looking around. "Every unit has something different, whether it be the color or the layout. Some have fireplaces, and some don't. So far, I've seen three units in this building, and they all have a different and unique feel to them."

"Oh, I guess. I didn't know that."

"And they hooked your unit up. I mean, the newer they are, the better they get. Man, I should have held out." He looked into the kitchen. "I know I would have gotten the stainless steel."

"What'd you get?"

"Black on black, which is nice, but I'd have opted for the stainless. At that time, though, it wasn't available."

"Oh, well, I guess I'm lucky."

"Yes, you are," he said.

She stood around while he looked around and made conversation. She was a little antsy. Tracy would be back at any moment, and although she tried to ignore it, he was the jealous type.

"Well, Jerome, I'm not trying to be a mean new neighbor, but I must get back to work."

Just then, Tracy walked in. "Hey, baby, I got—"

"Hey, man, what's up?" Jerome walked over to shake Tracy's hand. Tracy had the food in his hand, however, so he couldn't. Jerome put his hand down.

"Baby, Jerome lives across the hall. He came over to welcome me to the building," November said, taking the packages out of his hand and going into the kitchen.

"Oh, did he?" Tracy asked. He looked him up and down. "Looks like that's not all he came to do."

Jerome held up his hands. "Listen, man, I'm not trying to start no trouble. I was just checking out the features over here. You know, just seeing the difference in the amenities in this unit."

November could tell by the look on Tracy's face that he wasn't trying to hear him. "The difference how? Compared to what you have versus what you don't?"

"Yeah, you can say that." Jerome turned to November. "Well, Shareese, it has been a pleasure to meet you, and I'm sure I'll see you around. Take it easy, Tracy," he said and left.

"Yeah, man, later," Tracy said, shutting the door damn near on his heels.

"Tracy, what was all that?" she asked.

"You just moved in, and you let some stranger into your place, Novey? And then you got him calling you Shareese?"

"Hold on, Tracy, he is my neighbor, and I didn't want to be rude or seem unfriendly. And my name is Shareese. You are the only one besides my parents and coworkers who calls me November."

"Novey, what did you think I was gon' say when I walked in and saw Mr. Chocolate Chip up in my woman's face?" He walked to the kitchen where she was.

"Oh, now I'm your woman? Just before you were talking about if we make it. Now I'm your woman?"

"I didn't mean that. I mean . . . You know . . . you know what I mean, Novey."

"No, what do you mean, Tracy? I mean, because I don't wanna break any rules or misinterpret what we are, so please tell me, what do you mean?"

"Look, Novey, I care about you, all right? And I would like for us to be together, but I have to trust you. It's been a long time since I've felt this way about anyone, and if we are together, I need to be able to trust you. I want to be in a relationship with you, I do, but I have trouble trusting so easily."

"Have I given you any reason to not trust me, Tracy?" she asked softly.

"Damn, November." He walked off.

She couldn't figure him out. What was he talking about? They were together every day. They had shared practically every evening and weekend together since they started kicking it. And they were on the phone whenever they were apart. Why would he not trust her? He had to know she wasn't seeing anybody else.

"Tracy, baby, talk to me. What is this about? What did I do to get you upset?"

"Novey, you didn't do anything. Listen, I want to be with you, and I want us to be together, but I have to be able to trust you. And you have to be sure that you only want me, because I need you to be faithful to me."

"Tracy, I will be. You are the one who's holding back on me. What are you so afraid of? You know I'm not trying to play you, and I know you know I care about you too, so what's with this 'if we make it'? Either you wanna have a relationship with me or you don't." She looked him in the eyes. "I wouldn't hurt you, nor would I lie to you."

Hell, Tracy was good to her, and he was the only man she had shared herself like that with. Why would she mess that up? He was sweet, romantic, kind, generous, and to top the cake, gorgeous as hell. A man with those qualities had no damn reason to be insecure.

"I believe you, Novey, and I know you mean that. You are beautiful, and I didn't want to rush into anything, or even get involved like this, but I can't fight it anymore. I didn't expect to fall for you so hard, but I did, and it is what it is."

"Well, Tracy, I didn't expect any of this either. I didn't expect us to get this close, but it happened, and I don't want to turn back. I want to be with you, but if you are not ready for a relationship, I am cool with that."

"Listen, I am ready. I want us to be together as a couple, not just friends, but I want you for me and only me."

"Are you sure?"

He smiled. "Yes, I am sure."

"So, we are officially a couple now? None of that 'friend' business when you introduce me?"

"Yes, yes, yes," he said and pulled her close.

"All right, then let's eat," she said and kissed him.

"Okay." He followed her back into the kitchen. "And, Novey," he said.

"Yeah, baby," she answered thinking, *what now?*

"I don't wanna see Jerome's ass over here checking out your 'features and amenities' ever again."

"Okay, man, damn. I see how jealous you are."

"That's right," he said and popped her on the ass. "Because these are my features and amenities and Jerome doesn't need to be checking them out."

Chapter Nine

Life was good for November. She was settled into her new condo, and thanks to her man, she was pushing that Denali. It was hers not on loan, but in her name. Her life couldn't be better. Tracy had finally met her parents. She had been nervous about him meeting her daddy, but it had gone well. She was surprised because her dad never liked any of the guys she had brought home before.

When April met him, they hit if off from the start. November guessed it was because her sister was so bizarre. She had Tracy laughing all the time at her crazy ass. He told November that her sister was definitely a bit extra and she agreed. She knew that was his nice way of saying her sister was a loony tune.

They went over to her house for dinner one night and April, crazy-ass fool, convinced Tracy to let her tell him his future. She said some things that made his brow rise about fifteen times, some craziness about him traveling all over the country and having thirteen sons and buying a farm. He laughed all the way back to November's condo on that one.

"Hey, Miss Shareese," Jerome said when he came out of his condo. November was in the hall trying to get into her door. She had a couple bags with more merchandise for her new place.

"Hey, Jerome, how's it going?"

"Good. Do you need any help?"

"Nope, I'm good," she said, finally getting the door open.

"And you're also looking good," he complimented her, flirting with her again as he always did in passing.

"Thank you," she said, trying to get on the other side of her door.

"So, when are you gon' stop over to see my bricks?" he said, damn near following her into her unit. That made her nervous.

"Soon, real soon," she said, trying not to let him enter. Tracy was on his way, and the last thing she wanted him to see was Jerome in her condo.

"Well, how about now? I'd love to show you."

"Well, now is probably not the best time."

"Why? It'll only take a couple of moments. You have to see the craftsmanship on the cabinets and fireplace," he said, insisting.

"Okay, but I only have a minute." She pulled on her door but didn't shut it all the way, then followed Jerome across the hall. He was right. His place was absolutely beautiful. She looked around, admiring his décor, and he offered her a drink.

"No. No, thanks. I really should be going," she said, heading for the door.

"Already?" he said, standing close to her. He was making her feel uneasy.

"Yeah, Tracy should be coming any minute." She tried to move past him.

"Oh, yeah, the tow truck guy, right?" he asked as if her man's job was a fry cook at McDonald's.

"Yes. He owns two locations. You've heard of it, right? Stone Cold Towing?" she asked, knowing he probably hadn't.

"Oh, big man owns them, huh?"

"Yes, two."

"Ump, okay." His tone said, "Who cares?"

"So, I've got to be going," she said, trying to open the door.

He stopped her. "You sure you can't stay for a few more moments? I'd love to talk to you."

"I'm sure, Jerome. I gotta go." She walked out and saw Tracy approaching. "Hey, baby," she said nervously.

"Novey, what's going on?" he asked, narrowing his eyes at her.

November's eyes darted from Tracy to Jerome. The foolish grin on her neighbor's face didn't help the situation.

"Nothing, baby. I was on my way in when Jerome asked if I wanted to see his place. It's beautiful. Do you wanna see it?" Her hands were shaking, and she knew that looked bad. Although it was innocent and nothing had happened, she envisioned the huge argument she and Tracy would have behind him seeing her coming out of Jerome's condo.

"No, I'd rather not see it." He spoke through clenched teeth.

"Well, Shareese, I will see you around," Jerome said with a smirk and shut his door.

November wanted to slap his ass.

"Baby, it's not what you think, I swear," she said as soon as she and Tracy were inside her place.

"Oh, so what am I thinking, November? Tell me what you think I'm thinking," he yelled.

"Baby, please don't yell, okay? Please?" she pleaded.

"Tell me the truth. Are you fucking around with this cat?"

"Baby, no. I just got in. See, these are the things I just brought in. I set them right here, and I left the door cracked. I promise you there is nothing going on."

"I'm not a fool, November. Don't try to play me!" he roared.

"Tracy, please lower your voice. I said it was nothing and that's what it was. Nothing," she said sternly. She wasn't going to keep telling him the same thing over and over again. He had to accept that she was telling the truth.

"Whatever! You wanna play games, find another brother to play games with. I'm out!" He headed for the door.

She ran and blocked the door. "No, Tracy, I will not allow you to walk out on me this way. You have to believe me. I'm not interested in him. And absolutely nothing happened."

"Don't play with me, Novey! I know what I saw."

"All you saw was me walking out of Jerome's condo, that's it. I just walked in this building when you and I got off the phone. How could I come up, come into my place with bags, and go fuck and shower and get completely dressed? Baby, I knew you were on your way over here. Why would I do that? How could I do that?"

"November, I can't deal with a liar."

"Tracy, come on, now. You are a smart man. Come on, please look at me. I said I'll never lie to you and I meant that, Tracy."

"Novey, don't ever lie to me. It will be a bad thing if you cheat on me. I wouldn't be able to handle that. I wouldn't be able to be with you if you did that."

"Relax, baby. I care about you so much and this relationship. You make me so happy, and I don't wanna mess up a perfectly good relationship for a few moments of pleasure with some dude. I'd be so sad if I didn't have you, Tracy," she said.

"Baby, I believe you. It's just when I saw you coming out of his place, and he had that sly-ass look on his face, I immediately thought—"

"I know, Tracy. I know what you thought, and I'm sorry. I mean, you have to know that we have something special. And you know me, Tracy. I am happy."

"I don't want to be insecure, but for me, please stay away from that cat. I know he is checking you and I don't wanna have to fuck him up, Novey."

"I gotcha, baby. Just hi and bye, that's it."

"Not even that," he said with a frown.

"Come on, Trey. I can't be rude if the man speaks to me."

"Okay, I can live with that."

"Baby, you have to stop overreacting and trust me."

"I do, Novey, but that punk-ass dude across the hall is the one I don't trust."

"I know, Tracy, but you have to trust me and know that I won't do that."

"I know," he said, pulling her close. "And I love you, Novey." He kissed her on the forehead.

"I love you too, baby. And you are the only man I have eyes for," she told him with a smile. She wondered if he realized he just said he loved her for the first time.

"You sure you ain't checking old Tyrese across the hall?"

"Man, please. Jerome ain't got shit on you."

"I can live with that," he said, and they laughed.

Chapter Ten

For November and Tracy's birthday, Trent had planned a birthday party. November spent the day preparing for it, and when she was finally ready to go, there was no Tracy. She paced, keeping an eye on the clock, and wondered what was keeping him. When she heard him at the door, she made a mad dash to open it and found him holding a huge bouquet of roses.

"Hey, baby," she said. She stepped aside to let him in.

"Hey. These are for you, birthday girl." He handed her the flowers.

"Thank you. These are lovely." She kissed him before heading to the kitchen to put the flowers in water.

"Are you ready to go?"

"Yes, I am, Mr. Late."

"Hey, traffic was crazy. And we can be fashionably late. It's our party."

"That is the main reason why we should be on time," she said. She went to the closet and grabbed her heavy coat.

"Baby, we are the guests of honor. We need to make an entrance."

"Yeah, we do, I just didn't want it to be a late entrance." She pouted.

He walked over and grabbed her by the waist. "Listen, we are good, and you don't have to worry about a thing, okay?"

"Okay," she said and gave him a warm smile. His gentle touch made her feel more at ease.

"You look fantastic, Ms. Lady."

"You looking good yourself, Mr. Stone," she said.

He moved into a pose. "Well, you know. I try."

"Stop it, silly." She slapped him on the arm.

He laughed. "Come on, let me help you into your coat so we can get outta here."

By the time they made it there, the party was already jumping. They walked in hand in hand and November felt like a star. She was displeased to see a lot of the females from Tracy's homeboy's party, but she didn't let it get to her. She just made sure to try to stay close to Tracy all evening. They danced and drank and had a good time.

"Hey, birthday girl," Jonathan shouted. He leaned in and kissed November on the cheek.

"Hey, Jonathan. I'm glad you finally made it."

"Yes, me too. This is for you." He handed her a gift bag.

"Thanks. But you didn't have to get me anything." November was surprised that he had gotten her a gift, but she was grateful that he did. Jonathan was a cool guy. They got together from time to time—she, Tracy, Jonathan, and whoever he'd be dating at the time—so she thought it was sweet of him to bring her a gift.

"Why not? That would have been messed up for me not to bring a pretty lady a gift on her birthday." He smiled at her.

"Only if he got her man one too," Tracy said, walking up on their conversation.

"Man, come on. You know that would have been a bitch-ass move to get your ass a gift. But happy birthday, man. Your drinks are on me." He gave Tracy a brotherly hug.

"Yeah, dawg, you're right, but next time, don't buy my woman one neither. You feel me?" Tracy's face had no trace of a smile.

"Aww, Trey, man, come on. You know ladies live for gifts and shit. Don't trip, man, it was just me being a gentleman."

"Yeah, whatever, dude." Tracy pulled November close to him and wrapped his arms around her waist as if to prove his point.

"All right, dude. I'ma go get me a drink. Enjoy your party." Jonathan walked away shaking his head.

November turned to face Tracy. "Tracy, baby, calm down. It's not a big deal. Jonathan was just being nice."

"Look, I'm cool, but he knows not to be buying another man's woman a gift and shit."

"Tracy, it's a birthday gift. Not a 'hey, I was thinking of you, so I got you this' gift."

"Yeah, okay," he said.

November put the gift on the table with all of the other gifts, and they went back to their party. A little later, Jerome, November's neighbor, came in with a huge bouquet of flowers.

Why in the hell would he do that? November immediately wished that she hadn't invited his ass.

"Happy birthday, beautiful," he said. He handed them to her and gave her a friendly hug and a kiss on her cheek.

"Thank you, Jerome. These are nice." She looked around for Tracy.

Before she could say another word, Tracy had grabbed her arm, squeezing it, and he pulled her to the side. "What the fuck is he doing here?"

"I invited him, Tracy, and why you grabbing on me like that?" she asked, snatching away.

"You know I wouldn't want him, of all people in the world, here."

"Tracy, that shit is so old, and he is an okay guy. I saw him in the hall a few days ago. I mentioned us having a party, and he asked if he could come."

"And you knew I wouldn't like that," he yelled.

"No, I didn't think you'd mind. He ain't nobody, Tracy, and you hate him for no reason."

"Nope, that is where you are wrong. That motherfucker is a slick bastard, and you know I don't like him, Novey."

"Well, I don't like half of the chickenheads who are up in here either, but am I tripping?"

"What?"

"Yes. That ho who followed you outside trying to chase your truck down that time is here. I didn't think you'd invite her."

"I didn't, November. She must have heard about it through mutual friends. I don't know, but I didn't invite her." They continued to go back and forth until, finally, November decided she wanted to go home. He didn't continue to argue with her. He just took her home.

"Just pull over and let me out," November barked when they reached her building. She quickly unfastened her seat belt.

"Whatever, November," Tracy said.

"Then whatever, Tracy," she snapped back. She was ready to get the hell out of his truck, but he was trying to park.

"You know what? That is exactly how I expected you to act."

Her eyes narrowed. "Excuse me?"

"You act like you don't see anything wrong with this bullshit."

"No, Tracy, you act like this with every man who says hello to me. Like I don't have any self-control and I'm gon' just let some dude whisper in my ear and make me spread my legs and cheat on you!"

"Because that is what women do, Novey. They let cats grin and smile in their faces and tell them all kinds of bullshit, and then what? They end up bent over for some dude who doesn't give a shit."

"And you think I'm capable of that?"

"You know what? You could be. I don't know," he said.

That answer took November by surprise. She loved him, and he knew that, so how could he say that to her?

"You know what, Tracy? This ain't working out. This jealousy thing you've got going on is getting on my damn nerves. If a man says hello to me, you're clenching your fists, and I have to explain myself over and over. I'm tired of it."

"Oh, so we're through?" he asked.

She wasn't sure if that's what she meant, but she had been dealing with him and his overprotective, controlling ways and his jealous rages for too long now. It was making her insane.

"If you can't stop being so insecure and going off every time you see me talking to a man, yes."

"Well, fine!"

Tracy looked straight ahead and not at her. She sat there, hoping he'd take it back and say he would stop acting like an insecure lunatic, but after few moments of silence, she knew they were done. She got out and walked into her building, hurt and confused. She wished she hadn't invited Jerome. She wished Jonathan had never bought her a gift, and she wished she had never told Tracy that it wasn't working out. She loved him and wanted to be with him. She just wanted him to stop acting so damn jealous.

By the time she got to her door, she was angry. She looked at Jerome's door and wanted to throw eggs at it, but she knew he wasn't her problem. She went inside, and after she locked the door, she went to the phone. She called Tracy, but he ignored her call. She peeled off her boots and stripped down to her panties and bra. There was a tap on her door, and she dashed to it, just knowing Tracy had come back to talk to her.

When she opened the door and saw Jerome, she closed the door quickly. She grabbed her robe to cover her underwear, and when she opened the door again, he was about to go into his condo.

"Damn, baby, I thought you were expecting me a couple of seconds ago," he joked.

"Go to hell, Jerome," she snapped. She tried to close the door, but he stopped her.

"Hey, hold on. Hold on, Shareese. Please, I just wanted to say sorry for ruining your evening. I had no idea that your man would trip like that over me coming."

"Well, it's not your fault. It's my fault for inviting you."

"No, I know how dude is. I just should not have come."

"Well, it don't matter. We are over."

"No way. Because I came?"

"Don't flatter yourself, Jerome. There are other issues."

"Well, if it means anything, I'm sorry."

"Well, you know, that's the way love goes."

"Yeah, sometimes," he said and turned away.

She shut her door and went into her bedroom. She tried calling Tracy again, but he didn't answer. She looked at the clock and saw it wasn't even midnight. She thought for a moment. Why should she have had to leave her own party?

She got up and put her clothes back on, jumped in her truck, and went back.

"Where you been, girl?" April asked. "We've been looking all over for you."

November and Tracy's argument had been so horrific she forgot to tell her sister she was leaving. "Oh, I had to take care of a little girly emergency," she said, lying.

"Well, I am glad I found you, because we have to go. The sitter called and said Angel has a fever, so we are going to head home." She gave November a tight squeeze.

"Okay, just call me later. I hope she feels better," November said.

When April left, November hurried to find Tracy, because she figured he'd go back to continue celebrating without her, but she found Trent first. She wondered if he had talked to Tracy.

"Hey, Trent," she said nervously.

"Hey, birthday girl. Are you feeling better?"

"Huh?" November asked.

"Well, Tracy told me that you weren't feeling well and that's why he took you home."

"Where is Tracy?" she asked.

"Over there, I think. He is dancing," Trent said, pointing him out.

Tracy was on the dance floor, getting his groove on with some woman. November had a flashback of the movie *Two Can Play That Game* when Morris Chestnut was at the Budweiser party on the floor dancing with those women in front of Vivica Fox.

"Aww, hell naw," she said and walked up to him. She tapped him on the shoulder. "What are you doing?"

He turned to her, his eyes wide. "Novey—"

"Yes, Novey," she said sharply.

"Humph. Is there something wrong?" asked the female he was dancing with.

"Yes, there is," November spat, ready to get in her face if she wanted some.

"Novey, look, this isn't the time. Don't make a scene."

"Aww, Mr. Embarrass Me All The Damn Time doesn't want me to make a scene. I'll tell you what: I don't give a shit. Party on. Do whatever you like. Happy birthday!" she yelled and stormed away.

He called out her name, but she kept walking. She went over to the bar and got a shot of tequila, and then another and another. She was going to enjoy her birthday party with or without Tracy. They were done anyway. She wasn't going to let her night be a waste.

She danced and partied and did the damn thing until three a.m. By then, she was drunk and tired as hell. She hadn't seen Tracy since she had given him the finger from the dance floor. She had made her way to her truck when she heard a familiar voice call out her name. When she turned around, she saw Jonathan.

"November, are you okay?" he asked.

"I'm fine," she said, holding on to her door handle to keep from falling.

"You don't look fine. Are you sure you can drive?"

"Yeah, I can drive to St. Louis and back," she slurred. Although she was drunk, she knew she was going to have to pray to make it all the way home.

"Look, I'd be happy to drive you home."

"No, no, no," she cried, trying to hit the right button to unlock the door.

"Come on, November," he said, grabbing her hand.

"No, Jonathan. Tracy would kill me if he knew you were taking me home."

"Look, November, Tracy and I have been friends since we were five. He will kill me if I let you drive home like this."

"No, no, Jonathan. I'm fine." Tears burned her eyes.

"Shhhh. Come on, November, let me get you home." He took her hand and led her over to his Hummer. After he helped her into the passenger's seat, he hopped into the driver's seat and pulled out of the parking lot.

"I love him, Jonathan, and all I want is to make him happy, but he is so insecure, and I'm constantly trying to prove to him that I am faithful. Do you know he calls me almost every twenty minutes to confirm where I am and who I am with? I thought it was cute at first, but now I don't know. It is out of control. Why, Jonathan? Why does he act like that?" she asked, crying.

He reached over and grabbed some Kleenex from his armrest and handed it to her. "Well, November, Tracy wasn't always like this. He was the coolest, cockiest brother at one time. There was a time when he didn't get involved with, nor did he get close to, any woman. He used to keep a couple of chicks at a time, and he would always say women were scandalous and couldn't be trusted.

"Then he met this one chick named Brianna, and he changed. All he did was talk about Brianna. 'Bre this' and 'Bre that' was the only thing that came outta the brotha's mouth. They went on strong for about two years, and Tracy was in mad love with Brianna. Then, after all of that, he catches her with this dude, and that sorta messed him up. On the rebound, Tracy started talking to Ana, this chick we knew. She always had a thing for our boy Mike, but Mike was on some ol' bullshit, and he kept playing around. So she hooked up with Tracy. And after a little while, news got around to Mike that Tracy was kicking it with his number one fan, so he got his act together. And the moment he stepped to Ana, she bounced.

"Then, after about four years of him being single and not trusting women, he meets you and he falls for you, so he may be a li'l bit insecure. So if he is overprotective and has hang-ups, it's not because of you. I remember him saying that, after Ana, he would never love another woman or get close to another woman. And then you came along and made him eat his words. He loves you," Jonathan said, and she was quiet. She cried silently, but listened.

When they made it to her place, he tapped her leg to wake her because she had drifted off to sleep. He helped her up to the third floor and into her condo, and he made sure he locked her doorknob lock behind him.

She woke up the next afternoon around one thirty with a dry mouth and her head doing a drum solo. She rolled over and was happy to see that she at least had enough sense to remove her coat before lying down. Her keys and her purse were alongside her body. The night before must have been a lively one, because she had never gotten so drunk that she couldn't drive. She'd have to thank Jonathan for helping her home and inside her condo. She then remembered it was he who took off her coat. She'd barely been able to stand up.

Her horrible hangover was evidence that she had overdone it, and she felt like shit. She managed to sit up, and when she caught a view of herself in the dresser mirror, she almost screamed. *Who in the hell is that?* was her first thought when she saw her hair standing up on one side of her head. Dark makeup tracks were proof that she had been crying before passing out.

She pulled off her boots and let each one thump the floor. She got up and went into the kitchen to coat her throat with some orange juice, then she went through her purse for Excedrin to relieve her banging headache. She looked over at the phone and saw her message light blinking.

"Damn," she said out loud. How did she get so messed up and not even hear her phone? She went to her purse and looked at her cell phone. She had thirteen missed calls.

She decided to go to the bathroom before she listened to her messages. She had just started the shower running when she heard someone at the door. Yelling for whoever it was to give her a minute, she turned the water off, grabbed a scarf, and tied up her hair. She didn't want to go to the door looking like she'd just had a fight. She looked through the peephole and saw a delivery guy with roses.

She opened the door and offered him a tip, but he declined. She set the roses on the counter and opened the card. It was from Tracy.

My Sweet November,
You are the best thing to ever happen to me, and I do realize what I have with you. I am so sorry for being a jerk last night and ruining our party. We seriously need to talk. Please call me.
Tracy

She smiled and reached for the phone.

He answered on the second ring. "Novey, look, I'm so sorry for being an asshole last night."

"Good afternoon to you too," she said.

"Oh, baby, my bad. How are you?"

"Well, a little jacked up. I overdid it last night," she said, reaching for her glass of juice on the counter.

"Yeah, I saw you trying to be grown before I left."

"Yeah, I got my party on, that's for damn sure," she said. They both chuckled. "I got the roses, Tracy. They are just as beautiful as the ones you gave me yesterday."

"Well, you deserve them. I'm just happy that you called. We need to get together. I have some things I wanna say to you face-to-face. And I want to give you your birthday gift."

"Yeah, I need to give you yours too." She looked over at her dresser and realized it was still in her truck.

"So, can you come over so we can talk?"

"Yeah. Ummm, I mean, no," she said, remembering her Denali was still downtown, parked in the hotel's garage. She cringed when she thought about how much she was going to have to pay for parking.

"No? Why?"

"My truck is still downtown. I was a little too messed up to drive," she said, not wanting to tell him she had to get a ride.

"How did you get home?"

She really didn't want to answer that question. "Michelle," she said, lying. "You know, from the office?" She didn't want to have to explain Jonathan bringing her home. He would have another episode.

"Well, get ready, and I'll come and get you. We can get a bite and talk."

"Okay, but I need about two hours, because I have to do something with my hair."

"Okay, that's fine," he said.

Chapter Eleven

November jumped in the shower and shampooed her hair. She hurried to her closet to find something to wear so she could set under the dryer for a while. She had to try to get back to gorgeous like she had been the night before, she thought as she endured the heat from the dryer.

She texted Tracy and told him to give her a little more time because her hair was taking forever to dry. He responded, telling her to just text him when she was ready.

She put on a low-cut gray knit sweater and her sexy black jeans and gray boots. She admired herself in the mirror after her makeup was done. She had put on a few pounds since she had been dating Tracy because, if he didn't do anything, he fed her well. Even so, in her size-fourteen jeans, she had it going on, and she was no longer intimidated by gorgeous women.

They hung around his friends more than hers because she didn't have any close friends.

Her best friend from school had moved away after college, and her coworkers were not exactly her speed, so April was the only person she spent time with. She did family gatherings and hung out with a few of her cousins on occasion, but she never felt insecure around them with Tracy. Her cousins knew she'd beat a bitch down over her man.

She blotted her lips, did one last mirror check, and texted Tracy that she was ready. While she waited, she prayed to God to let the weird hangover feeling go away. Her headache was finally fading. Excedrin was her magic pill for headaches, and it had never let her down.

When Tracy knocked, she went to the door and opened it. He was looking as good as he always did. "Hey," he said, greeting her with a hug and a kiss. "Damn, baby, you are wearing those jeans."

"You like?" she said, turning to the side and doing a little pose.

"Oh, yeah," he said.

She couldn't help complimenting him too. He dressed so damn nice, and with him being over six feet and built, he looked nice in almost everything he wore, even his uniform.

"I try," he said, taking her compliment as he shut the door. He sat down, and she went into her bedroom to put on her jewelry and perfume.

She grabbed her leather jacket and matching purse and was ready to roll.

"So, are you ready?" he asked.

"Yeah. Let me just use the bathroom and we can go." She didn't know where they were going and she didn't want to have to rush to the bathroom when they got there.

"Okay, I'm all set," she said when she returned. She put on her coat.

They rode downtown to Socca for an early dinner and drinks. She was in no mood for anything heavy, so she decided to stick with iced tea. Tracy ordered a bottle of champagne, and she didn't want any, but he insisted she have a glass. She sipped it slowly, making sure she didn't make herself sick.

After a while, she went to the ladies' room for a moment to get away from drinking. She had drunk so much the night before, the champagne was making her feel woozy. She got back and took her seat and took a small sip. When she looked over at Tracy, she found him staring at her.

"What is it?" she asked.

"Nothing," he responded. "You are just amazing."

"So are you," she said and took another baby sip of her drink.

"Listen, Novey, I know that I have been trip-ping out, and sometimes I bug out, but I love you, and I am sorry for the way I've been acting and treating you. I don't want to push you away. I don't want to lose you."

"Tracy, I love you too, babe, and I'm not going anywhere. We can work this out."

"I am trying to deal with my issues of trust, okay? I know it is not you, and I do trust that you are here with me because you wanna be here with me. And I do believe that you wouldn't play me. I have no reason to not trust you. It's just sometimes . . ." He stopped talking and sighed.

"Listen, Tracy, I love you. I never thought that I would fall for you as hard as I have. You have to trust me and believe me when I say that I am here for you and only you."

"I do. That is why I got this." He opened a jewelry box with a diamond in it.

November put her glass on the table and tilted her head. She leaned forward to make sure her eyes were not deceiving her.

"November, I believe in my heart that you are sincere and that you are the only woman for me. I love you so much, and if you would accept this ring and be my wife, I will be the happiest man on this earth, and I promise that I will do my best to make you happy every day."

November was floored. She didn't know what to say or how to respond. She hadn't seen this coming. She was speechless at first and then she found her voice.

"Oh, my goodness. That's for me? Tracy, are you serious?" she asked with her eyes wide open.

"Yes. This is your birthday gift. I wanted to give this to you last night at the party and make it a big birthday/engagement celebration, but that didn't go smooth, so I'm asking you now. Will you marry me?" he asked.

November covered her mouth to keep from yelling out a yes. She couldn't believe this was happening to her. She tried to hold back the tears, but she couldn't.

"Tracy, you'd better mean this, because if I say yes, that's it. I mean, no take-backs."

"Yes, November, I mean every word." He held the ring, waiting for her answer. She sat for a moment or two trying to take it all in. "So, what do you say, November? Can you give me the rest of your life?"

"Yes, yes, yes," she said between sobs. She wanted to shout it at the top of her lungs. She knew that she loved him and wanted him in her life, but she hadn't thought he loved her enough to want to marry her.

"Yes, yes!" he yelled and slid the ring on her finger. They kissed, and November trembled. She couldn't stop shaking.

Tracy lifted his glass for a toast. "To us and a long and happy life together," he said. They clinked glasses.

November wiped her tears. She couldn't wait to tell her sister. What would her parents say?

The server refilled their glasses, and they sat hand in hand for a while before they decided to leave. They still had to get November's truck from the parking garage. He took her over to the garage, and she followed him back to his loft. She called April from her cell phone to tell her the news. She was engaged to be married to the man of her dreams, and she couldn't have been happier than she was at that moment.

Chapter Twelve

"Hey, Shareese," Jerome said. They had run into each other at the mail center in the hall of their complex.

"Hey, Jerome, how are you?" she said. She concentrated on pulling out the mail that was packed tightly in her mailbox.

She had been at Tracy's loft since they had gotten engaged and she had stopped by to get some more things so she could go back to his place. He kept tabs on her every move, and he wanted to know where she was every minute of the day, but she loved him, and she knew he had trust issues, so she tried not to say anything to him about his problem. She felt smothered at times, but she also felt good because he loved her so much.

"Good. I haven't seen you around much. How are thi . . ." He stopped midsentence. "Oh, I see how things are."

"What are you talking about?"

"I mean that," he said, pointing to her rock. "You're marrying that psycho cat?"

"Tracy is not psycho, Jerome."

"Okay, whatever you say. That cat is crazy jealous, and if you marry him, trust, he ain't gon' change. He just may get worse, so I'll be watching the news for you," he said. He chuckled, but November found no humor in what he had said.

"My man is a little jealous, yes, but he loves me, and he is not crazy, Jerome." Her cell phone rang. The caller ID showed it was Tracy, so she said her good-byes to Jerome. "Listen, I'll talk to you later." She headed for the stairs.

"Hey," she said when she answered.

"Hey, where you at?" he asked first thing.

"I'm walking up the stairs to my condo."

"Why are you taking the stairs?"

"Because if I had gotten on the elevator, the call would have dropped."

"Oh. How much longer are you gonna be?"

"Not too much longer. I just need to go through my mail and grab some more clothes, and then I'll be on my way back," she said. She stopped, breathing hard from climbing the stairs. *One more flight.*

"Okay, then. Call me when you are on the road," he said.

"I will," she said.

"I love you," he said.

"I love you too," she said and ended the call. She walked up the last flight and made her way to her door. Inside, she put the stack of mail and her keys on the kitchen island. A minute or two later, her house phone rang. It was Tracy.

"Hello," she said, rolling her eyes. It was so obvious that he was making sure she was in her condo.

"Baby, I forgot to ask you what you wanted for dinner tonight."

"I don't care, baby. Whatever you cook is fine," she said, pulling out a bag from her closet.

"Naw, baby, I'm not cooking. I'm getting take-out."

"Oh, well, whatever is fine." She took a few items from her dresser drawer. She wanted to get done with getting her stuff, but he was keeping her on the line, and she knew it was to only make sure he didn't hear any background noises or any voices.

"How about pasta?" he asked.

"Pasta sounds great, baby. Now, let me go so I can finish."

"All right. Just hurry."

"I will." She hung up before he could say another word. She grabbed a couple blouses and pairs of slacks and got a few sets of undies.

She remembered to get another jacket and two pairs of boots. Her garment bag was full, so she grabbed a smaller tote and put her underwear in it, thinking she could manage carrying her jacket and boots to keep from making two trips.

Once she was done, she went into the kitchen and went through her stack of mail. She watered her plants and was ready to leave when he called her again.

"Hello, Tracy," November said, trying not to sound impatient.

"Hey, babe, I ordered Chinese food instead. Is that okay?"

"Yes, Tracy, that's fine."

"It will be here in about forty-five. Do you think you'll be back by then?"

"Yes, I was just about to leave."

"Okay, then. I'll see you in a bit."

"Okay, baby. I love you," she said, rolling her eyes. She adored Tracy, but sometimes she felt like he was insane.

"I love you too," he said, and she hung up.

She looked around to make sure she had everything. She grabbed her coat and put it on then got her tote, garment bag, boots, jacket, and keys and she was on her way to the door when the phone rang again. This time, she was going to have to cuss, she thought as she went back to answer it. She had everything in her hands to make her exit in one trip, and he was calling again.

She cringed and stomped across the hardwood floors, but she relaxed when she saw her sister's number on the ID.

"Hey, April," she said, smiling when she picked up.

"Hey, little sis, how are you?"

"Good."

"Where in the hell have you been? I've been calling you all week."

"Girl, at Tracy's. Why didn't you call my cell phone?"

"Chile, I don't know. I've just been trying to catch you at home. How is that fiancé of yours?"

"Fine, and crazy as ever."

"That's good. Well, I've got some news for you." April sounded like she was smiling. "But please don't say anything to Momma and Daddy."

"What, girl? What?" November asked, pulling back the stool and sitting at the kitchen island. She pulled her arms out of her coat and got comfortable.

"I'm pregnant!" April squealed.

"No," November said in disbelief.

"Yes, I am! I'm having a baby!"

"Get out, April. You done did it again?"

"Yep, we are pregnant with baby number four."

"Damn, April, can you wait for me to have one?" November asked, joking.

"Chile, you better get on board."

"So what did your husband say about this fourth baby?"

"Chile, he is happy. I swear that man trying to keep me on lock."

"Naw, April, I think you trying to keep him on lock. You don't have to be having all those babies," November said jokingly.

"Girl, stop. I love my kids, and my husband loves us. We ain't mad 'cause God keep on blessing us. We just hope we get a boy this time."

"Me too. I love my nieces, but it would be cool to finally have a boy in this family." November laughed.

They carried on and on, and before November realized it, an hour had gone by. Her other line rang, and when she saw Tracy's number on the screen, she stopped laughing. She had forgotten all about him.

"Hold on, April, this is Tracy," she said and hit the flash button. "Hello," she said.

"What the fuck are you doing, November?" he yelled.

"What?" she asked, confused and not sure how to respond.

"You should have been here by now. What the fuck is keeping you? You playing games with me?" he yelled.

"No, baby, my sister called when I was on my way out. She had some good news, and we just got to talking."

"That's bullshit, November. I know you on some sneaky shit."

"No, I'm not. She is still on the other line right now."

"You know what, November? You've got fifteen minutes to get your ass over here!"

"Tracy, what is wrong with you? I just told you I was talking to my sister."

"Fifteen minutes," he snapped and hung up.

November went back to the other line trembling, but she put a smile in her voice for April. "April, baby, let me go. My man is hungry, and he's waiting on me to get back so we can eat together."

"G'on girl. I'll talk to you later."

"Okay, girl," November said.

"And, Shareese, please don't tell Momma yet. I want to tell her."

"Your secret is safe with me."

"Thanks, sis. I love you."

"I love ya too, sis. Bye."

November hung up and rushed out the door and down the steps, where she ran into Jerome again. Why did she have to see his ass all the time?

"Shareese," he said, trying to stop her.

"Look, Jerome, I'm in a hurry. I will talk to you some other time." She huffed and rushed by him. She loaded her stuff in the truck and pulled out of her parking space with her hands still shaking a little. She didn't know what else to say to Tracy besides the truth. She couldn't understand why his mind would always go to negative things like suspecting her of cheating all the time.

Once she got to his building, she blew out a deep breath and got her things from the back seat. She felt a little better. She knew she hadn't done anything wrong, and it wasn't like Tracy would physically abuse her.

She used the key he had given her. She usually got in before him in the evenings after work, and he wanted her there when he got in instead of her going to her place and then coming back.

When she walked through the door, the place was dim. Candles were burning, and she could hear soft music playing. She put her things in the foyer and looked around for Tracy, but he was nowhere to be found. She took off her coat and hung it up in the closet. When she closed the closet door, he was standing behind the door.

She jumped. "Oh, Tracy, you scared me, baby."
He just stood there looking at her. "What, baby?
What is it? What's wrong with you?"

Still silent, he grabbed her face and started
kissing her hard. He was holding her so tight she
would have had to struggle to break free from
his embrace.

"Stop it, Tracy, you are hurting me," she
moaned, trying to back up from him. "Baby, stop
it. Stop, you're hurting me."

He finally let her go. "Take your clothes off,"
he demanded and started pulling on her sweater.

"Tracy, baby, what are you doing? Please, stop
this," she cried, pushing his hands away.

"Take your clothes off!" he instructed with his
jaws clenched tight. "Let me smell yo' pussy."

She wondered what in the hell was wrong with
him. He had never talked to her like that before
or in that tone. "Tracy, stop it. Stop. Stop this,
okay? Just stop it," she cried, pushing his face.
She moved toward the door. "What is wrong
with you?" she asked, adjusting her sweater.

He moved toward her, and she backed away,
getting closer to the front door. She was going to
leave and get her shit later.

"Look, Novey, you have to understand that you
are my woman. I am not a fool, and I will not let
you fuck around on me in my face and get away

with it. Now, take off your clothes and let me smell your pussy," he demanded again.

"No!" she yelled and grabbed the doorknob.

He grabbed her from behind and held her tight.

"You have to understand that it doesn't work like that. I am your woman, Tracy, and I love you, but you are not going to make me feel like trash because of your insecurities. I want you to let me go so I can leave."

Tracy held her tight for a few minutes and refused to let her go. He started licking her neck and squeezing on her breast hard. It felt good and bad at the same time. She loved Tracy, and making love to him was one of her favorite things to do, but to take off her clothes for him to sniff her was some old, crazy bullshit.

"Baby, please stop," she begged. "Why are you acting like this, Tracy? Why are you treating me like this?" She wanted him to relax and stop having these insecurities. He had no reason not to trust her. "Tracy, baby, please talk to me."

He stopped groping her and stood still, holding her tight. "Tell me the truth, Novey. Please tell me the truth," he begged her.

She turned around and looked at him. "Tracy, why are you so insecure? Why can't you trust me? I am with you all the time. When I'm at work or away, you call me back to back. Tracy, please,

I'm begging you to understand that I don't want anyone else but you. I love you so much, and I would never hurt you. I can't continue to live like this. 'Where are you? Who are you with? Be here in exactly ten minutes.' 'Now I'm in the car. Now I'm on the elevator. I will call you as soon as I'm in the car. Or upstairs.' If I run and piss first before I call you, I have to explain that two-minute gap.

"I thought I could live with it and I thought things would get better, but they are getting worse. Why won't you trust me? What do I need to do to make you trust me, Tracy?" She was in tears, and she was exhausted by him, but she just couldn't walk away.

Tracy stood there for a moment before he spoke. "Novey, I don't know. I mean, I tell myself over and over, 'November is a good woman, and she will never do anything to hurt me,' but as soon as I try to relax my mind, I can't. I don't know why I get so crazy and feel like some dude is occupying your time. I have trusted women, and they have fucking lied to me and cheated and I . . . and I . . ." He stopped and walked away.

November walked over and hugged him from behind. "Tracy, I know that you've been hurt before, and I'm sorry. I never had someone to hurt me. I've been cheated on, but not by someone I truly loved, so I have never been in your shoes. But I can't continue to pay for what somebody else did. I'm not her, and I want you to try to relax and give me a chance. I love you, Tracy. You are a beautiful person, and don't you think that I wonder about the women you come in contact with each day? I wonder sometimes myself because I know how good you are and some other woman would love to have you.

"But when those types of thoughts come to my mind, I shut them down. I just think about all the things you do for me and the time you spend with me and how you make me feel when we are together. That is how I get past my insecurities. I am not the sexiest or the most attractive sister out there, and when I see these slim, tight-bodied, model-looking chicks flirting with you, don't you think I wonder if you would or wouldn't? But if I let that control our relationship, I'd go crazy.

"So, thinking of you and how well you treat me and how I am always smiling when we are together is my peace of mind and security. You are my man, and you have to love me to treat me so well. And you have to know the same. Trust me, Tracy. Baby, please try to trust me. I can't live like this anymore. I can't. You have got to fix it because this is wearing me down, baby." She hoped she was getting through to him.

"Baby, I'm so sorry." He turned to her, wrapped his arms around her, and held her tight, crying. "I didn't mean to grab you like that. You know I would never hurt you. Please forgive me. I will never treat you like that again," he said, kissing her hands.

"You are the first woman I've ever loved like this, and I just keep thinking, 'As soon as I get comfortable, I'm gon' catch her doing some foul shit.' But you keep showing me a better person. I'm sorry for putting you through the drama and making you responsible for something someone else did. This is my issue, and I'm going to promise that I will control myself. Can you give me a chance? Can you be patient with me? I am going to change, November. I promise you, baby. Just, please, don't leave me. I'm so fucking sorry. Don't leave me, babe. Please," he begged. "I know I have to change. I can't lose you. I love you too much."

"Tracy, I'm here, and I will be here and give you a chance. You just have to mean what you say this time. We have talked and talked, and you keep promising me that you are going to change and I keep believing you. You have to really mean it this time."

"Baby, I promise. I mean it, Novey, and I love you so damn much. I love you, and I can't live without you."

"I love you too, Tracy, and I am here to stay," she said and they kissed.

Chapter Thirteen

Things improved between November and
Tracy. He showed enormous change in his behavior. He eased up on the calls and the questioning,
and November was able to breathe. It was weird
to her at first, because she was used to the back-
to-back calls and not being able to take a piss
without having to explain herself. She was able
to get things done and go from place to place
without checking in, and it felt pretty damn good.

Her condo was not lived in because she was at
Tracy's twenty-four seven. It still looked brand
new. All she did was pay the mortgage there and
keep up the utilities. She couldn't remember the
last meal she had cooked in her own kitchen.

Spring was approaching, and her sister was
blooming like the flowers and grass. She was
pregnant and glowing, and she was beautiful.
November was happy for April, and she found
it hilarious when she found out she was having
another girl. April's husband made it clear that

after this one he wanted to give it one more try for a boy. November just shook her head. She had no clue how they did it.

Work was good for November and business was growing, causing her to be at work later, which made her fiancé uncomfortable, but he maintained it well. She spent less time explaining and pleading, and she felt like their relationship was growing and had a good chance of making it. She didn't want to have to continue to put up with Tracy's jealous rages, and she thanked God that he had calmed down.

Summertime came, and it was hot and full of wedding talk. They had finally set a date. Her condo and his loft were on the market, and they hoped to sell quickly so they could buy their first home together. They were looking at houses that November thought were too expensive, but her fiancé acted like money wasn't an object. She tried to enjoy looking at the lovely houses Jonathan showed them, but the price tags had her concerned.

"Baby, we need to talk," she said to Tracy while he was doing his workout.

She wondered how her man, sexy and fine as he was, never once complained about her thick thighs and plump ass. When they met she was a solid fourteen, and she had gained a few pounds along the way, but he never said a word. Not that she was sloppy, but her body was far from tight.

She now claimed a size fourteen in some clothes and a sixteen in others, because her ass and hips were out of control. She still had a semi-flat stomach, and her waist was still good, but since she was getting married, she had vowed to work out with Tracy, but that day hadn't come yet.

"What's up?" he asked between curls.

"Come on, babe, I need to talk to you with you not working out."

"Give me five minutes," he said, and she went into the kitchen.

She sat at the table waiting for him so they could discuss their finances. He had never asked her about money, what she made, what she could afford with the new house, or what bills she would have. She took care of her bills at her condo, and he took care of his bills at his loft. She never asked him either, but since they had been engaged, he had been paying her truck note. He always paid when they went out to dinner, and he had her beauty treatment money on the night table every Thursday morning for her hair, nails, feet, and eyebrows.

He came out of the spare room where he was working out and joined her at the table. "So, what's up? What do you wanna talk about?" he asked, wiping the sweat from his forehead with a towel.

"Money," she said nervously.

"Money? What about money?"

"Well, we have been looking at houses, and they've been on the pricey side. Now, there have been some beautiful houses that Jonathan has taken us to see, but I know what I can afford, and even with me selling my condo, the stuff we've been looking at is way out of my budget." She opened a folder on the table in front of her. "Now, we've never discussed this, but this is what I make a year. This is what I have in savings, and this is what I have in my checking." She laid it all out in front of him. She wasn't embarrassed, because she did okay, but she was concerned.

"Wow," he said, smiling.

"Wow, what?" she asked, wondering if he was laughing at her.

"You are truly amazing, you know that?"

November frowned. "Why would you say that? What do you mean?"

"You are amazing because you are concerned about how you can contribute to our lives financially, versus 'my man gon' take care of me,'" he said, rolling his neck and snapping his fingers. November laughed. "This is exactly why I love you so much," he said, getting up and walking away.

November was confused and wondered where he was going. They hadn't talked about anything, and she wasn't finished.

He came back to the table with his briefcase. "Now," he said, opening the case. He shuffled through some documents and pulled out some papers. "Here we go." He moved the briefcase to the side. "First of all, baby, don't worry about anything. We are good. This is what I make annually," he said, pointing to a figure that was three times her salary. Her eyes widened. "This is what we have in the bank." He pointed to another figure on a bank statement and November thought she was going to fall out of her chair.

"What? How? I mean, what the hell? What are you doing besides towing cars?"

"Well, I have properties and investments, plus I own half of the dealership. My daddy started us young, and once I got my degrees, I chose to run the towing company versus real estate, and these other avenues," he said. "So, every month, we generate revenue from this and this and this, plus I get this from the dealership," he said, showing her more paperwork. He laid it all out, and November was shocked.

Tracy had a whole lot of money, and she'd had no idea. He was loaded. She knew he wasn't broke, but damn, he was good for a whole minute, and he could afford a house three times as much as the houses they were looking at.

"So don't worry about anything. I'm gon' make a piece of change when I sell this loft because the value has skyrocketed since I purchased it, even though the economy is in the toilet. I bought it years ago a lot cheaper than what it's worth now. After all the rehabbing in the area, this place was a steal, so we are good. You are going to have an amazing home, so stop acting like you don't like the houses we've been looking at. You've found an excuse not to put in an offer on every house we have looked at. And I know you loved the one we saw yesterday."

"I did, but all I kept wondering was how could we afford it."

"Well, stop worrying. Whatever house you want we are going to get," he said.

"Why are you so good to me? Why am I so special?"

"Because you are." He caressed her cheek.

She smiled. "Well, since you got this, I can go shopping."

"Yes, if you want."

"Yes, I want. Man, I've been watching every dime here lately, wondering how I was gon' help you with these damn near million-dollar homes you've been showing me."

"Yeah, I can see why," he joked, looking at her bank statement on the table.

"Shut up!" she said and popped his arm.

"I'm just playing," he said, and they laughed.

"I just can't wait 'til I sell my condo."

"You will soon. Jonathan is a good agent. He will have us both sold in no time so, baby, we have to find a house."

"I know, but first things first. We still have to finish these minor details for our small but elegant wedding."

"I thought that was all done."

"Me too, but my momma keep on saying just one more person, just one more person. You know I wanted it to be intimate, Tracy. I don't want all these people she keeps adding to come. This is getting out of control."

"Well, just tell your moms not to invite any more people."

"Are you crazy?" she said, looking at him like he had lost his mind. "*You* call and tell her."

"Well, on second thought, just order more chairs and more food."

"Yeah, whatever. I just can't wait to do it."

"I can't wait either, my love," he said, putting his papers back into his briefcase.

"Tracy, do you remember me telling you about wanting to get my own business?"

"Yes." He didn't sound interested.

"I still do, you know. Once we are married, I don't want to continue working at the agency." She had tried discussing the idea before, and he had always seemed uninterested.

"Well, we'll see. Just relax, baby. You got plenty of time to think about that. Once we get married, get settled in the house, and start a family, you are going to be so busy. Let's just see how it goes."

"I know, Tracy, but I worked so hard to get through school. I just want to run my own show, you know? I'm tired of getting disapprovals for my ideas or getting a no answer to something I know is a great idea. I feel like they are holding me back."

"I know, baby, but don't worry. It will work out."

"You sure?"

"Yep, don't worry." He got up to put his briefcase back and then headed back into the other room. When that conversation came up, he'd make an exit or change the subject altogether.

November sat there waiting for him to come back so they could talk some more, but after a few moments, she realized he wasn't returning to that conversation.

Chapter Fourteen

On moving day, November was sick as a dog. She didn't know if she had the flu or what, but she couldn't keep anything down. She had thrown up everything she had eaten over the last four days, her face was pale, and she was just so tired and weak.

"Baby, how are you feeling?" Tracy asked, touching her head.

"Aww, Tracy, I don't know what's wrong with me."

"You want some orange juice?"

"Yes, please." She put her head back down then turned and looked over at the clock. It was ten until nine. The fellas would be there soon to move her things from her condo to storage. Her unit had sold, and she had four days to move all her things out and get it professionally cleaned. She was supposed to be excited, but she was too sick to be happy. She sat up when Tracy came back into her room with the juice.

"Here you go, baby. Drink this," he said, helping her with her pillow. "When Trent gets here, I'll have him run you over to the loft, and once we get everything into storage, I'll be home to take care of you."

"Baby, no. I need to tell you what goes to storage and what goes to the loft," she argued.

"No, you are sick, and I can handle it. Whatever we take that we shouldn't, I'll get it out or buy it. You need to rest."

"Are you sure?"

"Yes, don't worry. Everything is everything," he said, smiling.

November managed to get out of bed and put on her sweats. She sat on the sofa wondering what in the hell was wrong with her. She reached for her phone and called her sister.

"Hey, April," she said.

"Hey, Shareese. You sound horrible, what's up?"

"Girl, I don't know. I'm sick as a dog. I've been throwing up, and I swear I've lost ten pounds."

"I thought you were moving today."

"Yeah, we are, but I can't do it. I am just so tired. I was wondering if you could come over and make sure they don't break any of my stuff."

"I would, but you know I'm about to pop any day now. What would I do if my water breaks?" she asked, and November laughed.

"Aww, April, I'm sorry, I just didn't think about that. How have you been feeling?"

"Tired and anxious."

"I can only imagine."

"So, what you gon' do?"

"I'm going over to Tracy's while they move my things. How about you waddle over to keep me company?"

"Well, I guess I could since the kids are with Tony and it is kinda boring. The house is so empty and quiet."

"Well, Trent will be here soon to drop me off."

"Why don't I pick you up?"

"That's cool. How long will you be?"

"About thirty minutes."

"Okay, call me when you are downstairs," November said and hung up. "Tracy," she called as loud as she could. She didn't have the energy to even yell.

"Yes, baby?" He came running to the sofa.

"Listen, my sister is gonna pick me up."

"I thought Trent was gonna take you."

"I know, but my sister is gonna come over and take care of me."

"How can she take care of you, Novey? She is nine months pregnant."

"She is pregnant, not handicapped."

"Are you sure? Because I can make the boys handle this and come take care of you myself."

"No, baby, April can take care of me. That's my big sister."

"Okay," he said, finally giving in.

November waited for her sister to call, and when her phone rang, she told Tracy she was leaving.

He came out to give her a kiss. "Call me if you need anything," he said.

"I will, babe."

"I love you, and as soon as we are done, I'll be right home."

"I love you too," she said, and they kissed again.

She went down on the elevator, and she hated that she didn't take the stairs. The ride made her feel more nauseated, and when she got to her sister's SUV, it showed.

"Oh, girl, you look bad," April said when she got in.

"Gee, thanks, April," November said, rolling her eyes.

"No, I didn't mean anything by it. I'm just saying you look like I did when I was pregnant with Angel."

"What?"

"I mean, I looked pale and lifeless too for the first few weeks. Only with Angel, though. None of my other babies, just her."

"Well, I'm not pregnant," November said defensively.

"How do you know?"

"Because I know. Tracy and I take precautions."

"So are you on the pill?"

"No." November fidgeted in her seat.

"Condoms?" April asked.

"No, April. Damn!"

"Then, what do you use, Ms. Precautions?"

"The gel." November put her head back.

"A spermicide? Chile, you know that that mess is not one hundred percent effective, right?"

"It's been working since we've been together, my love."

"Well, maybe the last time y'all didn't use enough, because you look pregnant."

"How do I look pregnant, Cleo?" November asked, making fun of her. Her sister, the psychic wannabe, was at it again.

"Because I can tell. And we are going to stop at this Walgreens to get a test."

"No, we are not, because I just have the flu or a virus or something. I'm not pregnant, April."

"Yes, you are. You don't have no damn flu. Summer hasn't ended, and it is definitely not flu season, honey." April pulled into the Walgreens parking lot and found a spot.

November folded her arms. "I'm not getting out."

"Fine, stay in the truck. I'll get it myself."

November watched her sister waddle into the store. Her sister was a basket case. No way was she pregnant. She hadn't missed her period, and she didn't feel pregnant. She didn't know what pregnant felt like, but she knew she didn't feel like a pregnant woman.

April got back in the truck and tried to hand her bag to November, but she sat with her arms folded and wouldn't take it. Her sister shook her head and put it on her lap. They rode all the way to Tracy's with November's arms still folded. She refused to touch the bag holding the pregnancy test.

When they got inside, April bugged her and bugged her to take the test, but she refused. "Why are you so scared to take the test? If I'm wrong and you're not pregnant, then you're not pregnant. So why are you scared?"

"I'm not scared, April. I just cannot be pregnant two months before my wedding. That is not how it was supposed to be."

"Well, shit happens."

"Look, give it to me." November snatched the test out of April's hand. "I'll take this stupid test, just so you can know that you are not psychic, you nutcase." She marched into the bathroom, peed on the stick, and set it on the vanity. She washed her hands and looked at the spinning hourglass on the test and walked away. She opened the door and found April standing there.

"So?"

"It's still processing. I don't want to look at it process."

"Well, I do," April said, walking into the bathroom.

"Knock yourself out." November went into the kitchen to get some water. When she heard her sister scream, she rushed back to the bathroom. "What? What is it, April? Are you in labor?"

"No, silly, but you will be in about nine months." April held up the stick. It said PREGNANT in the little window.

November thought she might pass out. "No fucking way!" she yelled. She snatched the test from April's hand to get a closer look.

"I told you. I told you," April sang.

"Why are you so happy? This isn't good, April. Tracy is gonna go through the roof."

"Why? You are pregnant. That isn't such a bad thing."

"Yes, it is, April. We aren't married yet."

"So? You're getting married, what, in six or seven weeks?"

"How do I tell him I'm pregnant?"

"Easy. You say 'Tracy, you're gonna be a daddy.' That's exactly what I told Anthony the first time."

"Anthony is different. He wants you to have a team. He let you open a freaking daycare. He loves kids, but Tracy and I don't talk about kids. Maybe once or twice, but not much."

"Well, you gotta tell him, Shareese. You can't not tell him."

"I'm gonna tell him, but what if he gets mad and breaks off the engagement?"

"Why are you freaking out? Tracy loves you. Why would he kick you out because you are pregnant? Tracy wouldn't do that. He's not like that, Shareese, so why are you making him out to be this villain?"

"I don't know, April. I just didn't expect to get pregnant this soon. I wanted to get married, try to start my own business, and have a baby later on. Tracy and I didn't talk about getting pregnant right now, so I am not sure how he's gon' to react."

"Listen, baby, Tracy is a stand-up type of guy as far as I can see. He is going to be happy and so should you. Babies are a blessing. Not every woman can get pregnant, so God has put the baby in your womb for a reason, and that wasn't to destroy your relationship. So relax, it will be fine. Tell Tracy. He is going to be happy."

"You think so?"

"I know so." April gave November a hug.

The two women sat in the bathroom for a few moments while November shed some tears. She was emotional and nervous, but when she looked at the test in her hand, she smiled. She was going to be a mother. She was carrying Tracy's first child, and that made her feel privileged.

April stayed for a while, and they talked and talked until November felt better about the situation. After April left, she showered and put on some pajamas. She grabbed some crackers and poured herself a glass of ginger ale. April told her to eat small portions and try to keep crackers on hand 'til she got past the nausea stage. She ate slowly, trying not to piss the baby off so she wouldn't throw up again. After about thirty minutes, she felt better. The idea of having a little one was starting to sink in.

She got up and made a sandwich, praying that the little person had mercy on her and allowed her to keep it down. She looked in the mirror. Her color was coming back.

"Thank you, little one, for allowing Mommy to feel better," she said, rubbing her tummy. She had no idea what she was having or how far along she was. She went in the bedroom to take another nap because the act of eating the sandwich made her feel like she had run a marathon. She snuggled under the goose-down comforter and thought about the little being inside of her that had been draining every ounce of her energy for the past couple days. She drifted off to sleep and was awakened by a soft kiss on her cheek.

"Tracy, baby, what time is it?"

"After seven. How are you feeling?"

"After seven?" she said. She had been asleep since four o'clock that afternoon. *This little leech inside of me is gon' have me out for the count.*

"Yes, close to eight. We stopped and had a couple of beers when we were done," he said taking off his shirt. "How are you feeling, baby?"

"I'm feeling better. I managed to keep a turkey sandwich down."

"That's good, but if you don't feel completely better by tomorrow, first thing Monday you are going to the doctor's to see what's wrong with you." He took off his pants. He had on a pair of shorts, and he was looking delicious, November thought as she watched him move around the room.

"Well, Tracy, I am going to the doctor's on Monday, but I already know what is wrong with me."

"Okay then, what?" he said, digging through his drawer. November wondered what he was looking for.

"I'm pregnant," she said and lay still, awaiting his reaction. Her heart thumped against her chest, and she just wanted him to say something to let her know that the news was good news, and not bad.

Tracy paused. He tilted his head and just stood there with his back to her. She got nervous when he didn't say anything.

"Huh?" he said, turning to face her.

She swallowed. "I said I am pregnant."

"Did you say pregnant?" he asked.

November wished she could take it back. She sat up and looked down at her lap before she spoke again. "Yes," she whispered.

"Novey, don't play. For real?"

"Yes, for real."

"For real, for real?" he asked.

Her eyes started to well. "Yes, Tracy, you are going to be a daddy."

"Are you serious? I'm gonna be a daddy?" he yelled with excitement.

November was relieved. The tears were rolling then, but she nodded, answering his question.

"Oh, baby, that is fantastic," he said, moving close to her.

"You're not mad?" she asked, shaking like a leaf.

"Hell, no. Why would I be mad? We are having our first baby. Why would that make me mad, Novey?"

"I don't know. I didn't know how you'd respond."

"Happy, girl. Damn happy. How do you know? I mean, when did you know? Tell me how."

"April convinced me to do a test today, and it was positive."

"Aww, baby, this is great," he said, hugging her.

"You're really happy, Tracy?"

"Of course I am, baby. You are having my very first kid. I am more than happy. I mean, Novey, I love you. You are the best thing that ever happened to me, and you and I are going to make amazing parents. With my brains and your good looks, this kid is gonna be the man," he said, caressing her cheek.

"Hold on, partner, this could be a girl."

"Could be, but I know it's not. We Stones only make boys. Look at Trent. He has three boys. My daddy made two boys and I know I'm gonna have a boy."

"Well, Mr. Stone, we will see. I just hope we are settled and have the house by the time he or she arrives. I've always wanted to have a nursery."

"Oh, we will. Your condo is already sold, and it should be just a matter of weeks before the loft is sold. Before you are even showing, we should be settled."

"And I'm also glad we are getting married in a few weeks. Lord knows, I never wanted to be already pregnant at the altar."

"Well, my love, things happen for a reason."

"Yes, I know. And hopefully, Monday I'll find out how far we are, and we will know when this little leech is coming."

"Leech? Why would you say that?"

"The way I've been feeling lately, this baby is sucking me dry."

"Well, this is only the beginning." He kissed her forehead and then her neck, and made his way down to her breasts. He lifted her top over her head and smiled at her dark nipples. He leaned forward and kissed her tummy.

"Let me shower and get back to y'all," he said, rubbing it.

He headed for the bathroom and started the water. While he showered, he sang loud. November frowned at the horrible sound. He couldn't sing a lick.

When he came out of the bathroom, he had a towel wrapped around his waist. He still had water running down his chest, and

November wanted to lick it off. She watched him dry off and step into his boxers.

She smiled. "Why are putting those on when I'm about to take them right off?"

"Oh, it's like that?" he said, taking them back off.

"Yes, it's like that."

Tracy climbed into bed, and they started kissing. He licked her body, and as usual, reached over to get the contraceptive gel from the drawer.

"Why are you getting that?" she asked.

"Because," he said. He paused. "Oh, I guess we won't be needing this for a while, huh?"

"Nope, we won't," she said and smiled.

She reached over and turned out the lamp on the nightstand, and they shared another night of good loving.

Chapter Fifteen

It's so funny how time flies, November thought as she looked at her tummy. She was five months along and had already gained thirteen pounds. Her baby boy was doing fine, and they were looking forward to his arrival. Their new house was lovely. Painters were coming to paint the nursery.

She was elated until her domineering husband called and said he was on his way home. She knew it was because he didn't trust men in the house with her. She was so weary of his possessiveness that she didn't bother to put up a fight. She told him that if he wanted to be there, he should come home so he could be there.

She wondered why he would think a couple of painters would come on to a pregnant woman with swollen feet. She knew no one was checking her fat ass out, and she just couldn't understand why her husband didn't realize the same exact thing. He would swear that men at work wanted to get some of her pregnant pussy and she used to argue, but now she just agreed and told him that he was right whenever he suggested someone was checking her out.

The only places she could go really without questions was to work and April's, and sometimes she'd go insane there because of so many kids being there. Work was just work, and since Tracy had convinced her to go part-time, she didn't feel valued there, so she put all her energy into decorating her home.

She had always known one day she'd be married and become a mom, but never in a million years did she think her life would go the way it went. She never thought she'd marry a man who couldn't relax if she walked around the corner, and she damn sure thought her career in advertising would have gone differently. She found herself just being content and not happy, but she loved Tracy too much to leave him.

Tracy was a good man—kind, loving, attentive, and romantic—and the lovemaking was insane. She adored him, but there were times when she wished she would have left him a long time ago. Instead of giving him chance after chance to change, she should have been done. But she just couldn't walk away. Now, he was her husband, and the value of marriage meant so much to her.

She took her vows seriously, and she knew no matter what, she had to stick with it. She continued to pray for change, even more so now, since they were having a child. Single motherhood was not in her future, November declared.

She just wanted Tracy to relax and stop being so insanely jealous. He'd go through a period where he'd do well, but one event or situation would send him two steps back. She remembered a time when one of her coworkers invited her to a candle party that she was hosting and he insisted that he go with her.

She told him over and over that there wouldn't be any men there, but he insisted that she was lying and he wanted to go anyway. When they got to Sabrina's house and it was full of women, he felt foolish and told November to call him when she was ready. When it was over, another girl at the party offered to give her a ride home since she was going her way. She agreed instead of making her husband come all the way back to get her.

When she got home, Tracy wasn't there, so she called him to let him know she was home. He went ballistic. He hurried home and woke her up out of sleep in a rage, demanding to know what man had really brought her home.

She promised him it was a woman named Denise from the party and even offered to call her to prove that she wasn't lying to him. He had this big old scheme in his head of how, after he left, she had called her lover to pick her up, she went and spent time with him, and he had dropped her home. She was tired and didn't want to go through this again. She tried to show him how ridiculous he sounded, but he wouldn't listen.

"Tracy, I am carrying your child. I would never mess around on you. Especially while I'm carrying our baby."

"So if you weren't pregnant, you'd be with another man?"

"No, Tracy, that is crazy. I am not cheating on you. I will never do that to you. I can call Sabrina, and she can verify that Denise gave me a ride. I'll call her if you want me to."

He finally calmed down and went downstairs. November stayed in their bed and cried in the dark.

Tracy had been doing great before that night. That one incident set them back, and he was driving her crazy. She promised herself that she wasn't going to let him stress her out while she was pregnant, so from that moment on, she just went along with whatever he said without a fight. She let him take her everywhere and be under her if he wanted to. She didn't say anything about his back-to-back calls because she had become accustomed to him and his routine.

She loved Tracy, and she knew he loved her, but she didn't know how to help him. She didn't want to leave him, either, because he treated her well and would give her the world. Other than his jealous rages, things were perfect, and she knew she was blessed to have everything she had with him. The good did outweigh the bad, but she didn't know how much more of the bad she could endure.

She went downstairs to get a glass of water when he called her again for the second time in thirty minutes.

"Hello," she said.

"Hey, baby, how you feeling?"

"I'm fine, Tracy," she said and took a drink.

"Did the painters get there yet?"

"Nope." She put the glass down to rub her tummy because the baby was moving.

"Good. I'm on my way. I will be there in about ten minutes. I don't want those cats checking out my beautiful wife."

"Tracy, stop it. I'm almost six months pregnant, and I look like the Michelin Man. Ain't nobody gonna be checking me out," she said and went for a banana.

"Baby, don't say that. You are pregnant, not fat, and you are as beautiful as the day we met," he said with the same kindness and complimenting words he had used since they first started dating. He had his ways, but he never held back his love, and never did he stop going out of his way to make her feel beautiful.

"Why, thank you, baby. Sometimes, you say the sweetest things."

"You are welcome, Mrs. Stone. I mean every word I say. I am so lucky to have you."

"I'm lucky to have you too, babe, and you are the only man I will ever love," she said, trying to confirm she wanted only him.

"I know, November."

"Good," she said and smiled.

"I love you, and I'll be there in a minute," he said and ended the call.

Tracy got there about five minutes before the painters, and he made sure November made her exit after telling them the details of what she wanted. She held her stomach and shook her head as she walked out of the room. She had no idea what she was going to do to make that man get the idea of her cheating on him out of his damn head.

Chapter Sixteen

"Tracy, where are my keys?" November asked, looking around for them.

Tracy was lying on the couch taking a nap while she was going stir crazy. She was nine months and miserable. She had been in the house for days. She wasn't working anymore, and she needed to get out.

"I don't know," he grumbled and repositioned himself.

"Tracy, get up! Where are my keys!" she yelled and smacked his arm as hard as she could. If he didn't give her the keys, she was going to call a cab.

"Man, go on now. I'm trying to take a nap."

"Okay then, where are your keys?" she asked, going to the counter where he usually laid one of his sets of keys and his wallet.

He hopped up. "Why? Where are you trying to go, Novey?"

"Away. Anywhere, Tracy. I need to get out. I've been in this house for days. I've cleaned everything twice, I've rearranged the baby's bag forty times, and I've triple-checked my hospital bag. The plants are watered, the laundry is done, and the fish are fed. I need to get outta here. I need some air," she yelled.

"And go where, Novey? You are nine months pregnant, and our child could come at any moment now."

"Well, I don't think it's gonna be this moment. Now, I know you hid my keys like you always do," she said, moving in on him like she was going to punch him in the face. "Now give 'em to me! I'm tired of being a prisoner in my own home."

Tracy jumped up and grabbed her arms. She was hysterical, and she started to cry uncontrollably.

He looked scared. "Baby, calm down, please. Relax. I will help you find your keys, and you can go anywhere you wanna for as long as you like. But please, calm down. You are pregnant, and I can't let you leave this upset. You can take the Benz or the Infiniti if you want. I don't care. Just calm down, Novey." He held her while she sobbed in his arms.

"I'm so tired and frustrated. You never let me go anywhere. Why do you hold me like a prisoner? Why are you so, so insecure? I love you, Tracy. I only love you," she cried.

"Shhhh. Please, Novey, don't cry."

"I do everything for you, Tracy. I cook, I clean, I take care of you, and I'm home. I'm here. I'm home. I'm home for you, for everything!" she yelled. She was finally fed up. "I don't complain, and you still have this fear that some other man is gonna take me away. I'm tired. I don't want nobody else, Tracy. I promise you I don't! You can't keep doing this to me, you just can't. I don't wanna stay in this marriage if this is how it's gonna be.

"I want to be happy and free to go to the market without a million questions or a call from you on my cell phone every three minutes. People see us, they see me, and they tell me how lucky I am to have a man like you to love me so much, but I'm not. This is too much, Tracy, locking me in this house. I feel like I'm on house arrest, and I cannot take it another day. I wanna go, Tracy. I wanna go. Please let me go!" she begged. She sobbed uncontrollably.

Her head started to feel dizzy, and she had to sit down. The baby was moving frantically, and it scared her, so she knew she had to calm down and take a breath. She moved out of his embrace and damn near fell onto the love seat.

By the look of terror on Tracy's face, she gathered he was finally listening.

He knelt in front of her with tears in his eyes.

She lifted a hand and caressed his cheek. "You have to stop, Tracy. I'm miserable, and you have to stop treating me like this."

"I want to, but I just don't know how to stop. I don't know how to trust a woman completely, and I hate who I am, Novey. I hate that I'm ruining this marriage. Baby, I'm so sorry. Please calm down, baby, and breathe. Take a deep breath," he instructed.

He ran and got her a glass of water, and she took a couple sips and wiped her face. She took several deep breaths and began to relax. She had to, for her baby's sake.

"I can't do this anymore," she whispered.

Tracy went back to his knees in front of her. "Forgive me please, baby, please. I'm so fucking sorry, Novey. Please don't leave me. I'm begging you not to leave me. I'm gonna get some help, baby. It's not your fault. None of this is you; it's me. Please, I swear to you on my life, I will change. Just don't leave me," he pleaded.

November wanted to believe him, but she had heard that song before.

"I never meant to hurt you," he continued. "You gotta know that. You and my son are the only two things on this planet that I love more than anything. Please, Novey, I'm begging you." He looked sincere, but she still wasn't convinced. "I'll do anything to save our marriage. I will get some help, I promise. Please, baby." He put his head in her lap and sobbed.

She hated that she loved him so much at that moment because she truly wanted to tell him to kick rocks. But she rubbed his head and breathed out a sigh, hoping he would do what he said this time.

He looked up at November, and she wiped his tears. "Novey, I'll give you your keys. From now on, you can go wherever you wanna go, whenever. No questions. I know you are loving and faithful, and I'm sorry. Can you please forgive me for being an insecure fool?" he asked.

"Tracy, I love you, and I am trying to be patient because you are my husband and I want this marriage, but you've got to promise me that you are honest this time about getting some help. You've said this so many times before, and I can't continue to be here for you and love you if you can't do what you say you will do.

"I'm gonna trust you again, and I have faith that our marriage is gonna be fine, but please be a man of your word. I've heard the 'I'm gonna change' speech too many times, and I am ready to walk away to be happy and never look back.

Please do what you say," she said looking into
his eyes. She wanted him to know that it was
time for him to get his shit together.

"I hear you, Novey. I hear you. You'll see. From
here on out, things will be different," he said and
stood up. He went into the kitchen, reached over
the fridge, and got her keys out of the hiding
place he had them in. "Here, baby." He came
back and handed them to her. "Go out and get
some air. Take all the time you need. I'll be here
waiting for you." He leaned over and kissed her
forehead. "I love you so much."

"Thank you," she said, holding her keys tightly
in her hand. She stood up and got her coat. She
was serious about getting out of the house, and
although they had talked, she was still leaving for a while. "I love you too," she said and
headed for the garage. He sat down on the sofa
and didn't try to stop her from leaving.

The baby had finally stopped moving like
crazy, and she felt better already. Relieved, she
got into her Denali and let the seat back another
notch. She hadn't driven in a while, and she had
grown more since the last time she drove. She
cranked the engine and pushed the garage door
opener. She sat there for a few moments waiting
for the engine to warm up.

It was May, but the weather was still cold. She slowly backed away, thinking her cell phone was gonna ring or he'd come running into the garage to stop her, but neither happened. She drove down the block and smiled and thanked God for answering her prayers to get through to Tracy. She jumped onto the expressway and headed to see her parents. She hadn't seen them in a couple of months, and she knew they were going to be shocked to see how much bigger her belly had gotten.

When she pulled into the driveway, she saw her sister's SUV. She was happy because she hadn't seen April in a couple weeks. The usual family roaring was coming from the kitchen, so she walked in.

"Hello," she said, smiling from ear to ear. It was so good seeing them.

"Hey, sissy," April said, hopping off the stool and hugging her.

"Well, hello, stranger," her daddy said.

"Oh my goodness, look at you," April said, helping her out of her coat.

"Oh, my grandson sho' gon' be a big boy," her mother said, giving her a big hug. "Where is Tracy?"

"At the house. He was tired and on the couch napping. I was bored, so here I am," November said.

"Well, tell him we miss him too. Come on in and sit down. Let me fix you a plate," her momma said.

November took a seat next to April. She let her family fuss over her, and she enjoyed herself. To her surprise, her cell phone didn't ring one time.

Later in the evening, she was getting tired, so she got ready to head home. It had felt so good to get out to visit with her family that she smiled the entire ride home.

Tracy's Benz was in the garage, but his Infiniti was gone. She wondered where he was, but she didn't panic. When she got inside, she called him. His voice mail picked up. A couple minutes went by and then he called her back.

"Hey, baby," she said softly.

"Hey, my love. I see you made it in."

"Yeah, I got in about ten minutes ago. Where are you?" she asked for the first time. That question usually came out of his mouth.

"On my way. I ran out to get a bite, but I'll be there in about ten minutes. I will be honest, I was afraid you wouldn't come home."

"If I wasn't, I would have told you," she said, going upstairs so she could undress. She was full and tired and couldn't wait to get into bed.

"Yeah, I guess, but I was scared. I won't lie," he confessed.

"Well, I'm home," she said, stepping out of her pants. "And I can't wait until you get here. My lower back is killing me, and I need you to give me the magic," she said, talking about a massage. Tracy was good at giving them.

"I'm almost there, and when I get home, I'll give you the magic, babe," he said with a smile in his voice.

"Oh, okay. Ouch," she moaned. "Ooohhh," she said and stood still.

"What's wrong?"

"I just had a . . . Ooohhh. Awwww, Tracy, something ain't right." She moaned again.

"What is it, Novey?"

"I don't know. Maybe TJ didn't like the spices in the food I had at Momma's. Awwww. Oh, Tracy, I think my water just broke." Warm liquid ran down her legs. *Glad I'm in the bathroom,* she thought distractedly. *This would have made a mess of the carpet.*

"Hold on, baby, I'll be right there," Tracy said.

"Baby, I need to call April. I don't know what to do," she cried.

"Okay, but I'm on my way."

"Just hurry. I'm scared, Tracy," she said, panicking. She hung up and dialed April.

April tried to calm November down, but she was so scared and wouldn't listen to April because her contractions started coming on strong and fast.

Tracy was there within minutes, and he helped her put on a robe and her coat. He drove to the hospital holding her hand and telling her to relax, but it was hurting so bad she couldn't get comfortable in the seat. She moaned and cussed the whole ride. By the time they got to the hospital, she was contracting every three minutes. It wasn't long before little Tracy made his way into the world.

"He is beautiful," Tracy said, holding his newborn son.

"Thank you," November said jokingly.

"What do you mean, thank you? I'm talking about the baby," he joked back with her.

"I know," she said smiling.

"I'm so happy right now, Novey. You did real good, baby. He is perfect. He looks just like you."

"You think so? I think he looks more like you."

"No, look at his eyes. He has your eyes."

"And the rest of him is you," she said.

They couldn't stop smiling. This was the best day of their lives. November had had a major breakthrough with Tracy, and her son was born. She smiled to herself. *I'm not doing too badly.*

Chapter Seventeen

Going back to work was hard for November. She had been off for almost a year, and going back to the company was not what she really wanted to do. She wanted to venture into her own thing, but Tracy had insisted that, if she worked, she could only do part-time at the agency. Although he wanted her to be a full-time mom instead, he compromised by letting her go back part-time. She had a hard time leaving her baby, but she felt at ease because he went to April's daycare center, so she knew he was in good hands.

Tracy was busy with other avenues of business. He had opened an auto repair shop, and he was busy and gone most of the time. She was so proud of him because he was a changed man. Her cell phone calls from him were normal, and there were no more prison stories. She was finally living a normal life, and she was happy. Her little boy was going to turn six months old that November, and he was their joy.

She had lost a few pounds and was actually a bit smaller than she was before she got pregnant, so she was on cloud nine. When she left the office, she called April to let her know she would be late. She wanted to stop by the grocery store to get a few items. When she was walking to her new Escalade, she got a weird feeling that someone was following her.

She turned and saw a man a few feet away, so she loaded her bags as fast as she could and pulled out her cell phone to call Tracy so she could have someone on the phone in case the stranger was someone she should worry about. She wasn't in the mood for anyone trying any funny business, so she wanted to let Tracy know exactly where she was, just in case she came up missing.

She was disappointed when she got his voice mail, but she started talking like she was carrying on a conversation until she was safely inside her vehicle. She pulled out of the parking lot and took a deep breath, but she looked in her rearview mirror and could have sworn the same car was following her earlier. She drove to her sister's and went inside. She was a bit shaken from the parking lot experience, so she sat and talked to April for a while before she left.

At home, she put the baby in his swing and changed to start dinner. She cranked the music and poured herself a glass of merlot. She had missed drinking wine and any other liquor while she was pregnant, and now she was no longer breastfeeding, so she sipped her wine like it was the best-tasting liquid in the world. Less than an hour later, her loving husband walked in and greeted her with a nice kiss.

"Hey, baby. Ummm, you got it smelling good up in here," he said, opening the cabinet. He took out a glass and poured himself some scotch. "Where's my little guy?"

"Over in his swing. Dinner will be ready in a few minutes," November told him.

Tracy moved to TJ. The baby was excited to see his daddy for sure because he talked up a storm. November knew he was happy to be coming out of his swing and moving around. It was hard for her to cook with him sometimes because he'd cry for her to hold him. She'd give him animal crackers and his favorite toy to occupy him while she fixed dinner.

Tracy walked back into the kitchen, and she realized he wasn't in his towing uniform. "Hey, where have you been in those nice clothes?"

"I had some other business to take care of. How was work for you today?"

"Hard. I still haven't adjusted to being back or being away from TJ." When the words left her mouth, she wished she would have just said that things went fine.

"I told you, you don't have to worry about working, but you insist that you wanna work."

"No, I insist I want to open my own agency, but you're not trying to hear that," she said.

"Novey, please. I just got home, and I don't wanna discuss that right now."

"Why not, baby? You have all these good things going on, and you are opening businesses left and right, but for me, you won't."

"I never said I won't. I said not now." He got up and kissed her. "Come on, baby, let's not get into it. I'm in a good mood, dinner smells wonderful, and my son is ready for his daddy to get outta this suit and play airplane with him."

"Fine," she said, dicing tomatoes for a salad. It was no use trying to talk to Tracy about her business. She hated that he didn't take her seriously.

"And please drop the attitude, because I'm not going to change my mind. Our son is too little for you to take on your own advertising agency." Tracy walked over and picked up the baby. "I'm going up to change. I'll take TJ with me."

When they came back down, Tracy put TJ into his high chair, and they sat down and ate dinner.

The conversation was light, and November knew it wasn't a good idea to bring going into business for herself back up. She didn't want to cause another argument. She was just relieved that they ate dinner in peace.

She cleared the table and cleaned the kitchen and got the baby bathed and down for the night. Tracy was comfortable on the sofa with the remote in his hand. Their relationship was superb now that Tracy acted like a normal person instead of a jealous lunatic. She hadn't had to visit the jealousy conversation anymore since the night her son was born, and all she wanted now was for him to understand how much starting her own company meant to her.

"Hey, you want some company?" she asked, joining him on the sofa.

"Yeah, come and keep me company," he said.

She walked over and straddled him. She had come to give him a little more than company. She leaned over and kissed him softly on the lips.

"Aww, that's what time it is?" he asked, smiling.

She lifted her shirt over her head and undid her bra. "Oh yes, baby, this is what time it is."

Tracy reached up and cupped her breasts and massaged them gently. He sat up and took one of her nipples into his mouth. The warmth of his breath felt good, and she wanted him to suck harder. It hadn't been long since she had stopped breastfeeding, and she knew that's why he didn't suck as hard as she craved him to.

They kissed passionately, and she remembered why she had fallen in love with Tracy. He was a fantastic kisser and lover. She always got wet just from kissing him. He twisted her nipples, giving her the pleasure she couldn't get from him sucking on them so lightly.

He rubbed her ass while she ground against his crotch. His erection was like a pipe covered in cotton. She pulled his shorts down and pulled away his boxers and took him deep inside of her mouth. His groans and the pulsation of his body let her know that she was pleasing him the right way.

She enjoyed taking her husband's thick, smooth pole inside of her mouth. She clenched her jaws and carefully bobbed up and down, careful not to let her teeth get in the way.

He moaned and groaned, cheering her on to suck his dick right. He rubbed her hair. "Yes, baby, that's so good." Her spot ached and throbbed for him to be inside of her.

She stood and allowed her husband to pull her panties down. He put his fingers between her legs and rubbed her clit gently, causing her to become even wetter than she was.

"Oh, shit, girl," he whispered.

She pushed him back onto the couch, slid down onto his erection, and bounced up and down. When he pulled her all the way down on it, she rolled her hips.

Even after the baby, her silky tunnel was still a perfect fit for her husband's nine-inch instrument. She enjoyed the sounds of his moans as she rode him. She arched her back, allowing him access to her breasts, and he didn't waste any time taking one of her hard nipples into his mouth. It felt so good her moans were louder than his. He grabbed her ass and pushed up to get as deep as he could.

"Aww, yeah, Novey. Ride that dick, baby." When she exploded, he said, "Oh yeah, baby, that's it."

She rolled her hips harder, and after a few minutes of her giving him her best performance, he made her turn over. He laid her on her back and got on his knees in front of the couch.

Her ass was hanging off the sofa, and he put her knees over his shoulders. He plunged into her wet pocket, and she could hear the juices popping as he stroked her. His pumps went from steady to a fast, thumping pace. Their skin slapped, and she moaned and screamed from the pleasure he was giving her.

He leaned forward, putting his mouth on one of her nipples, and he sucked as hard as he could. His hot juice squirted out of his manhood, and he pushed it deeper inside of her. She rubbed his head and listened to his heavy breathing. He rose up and kissed her softly.

"Damn, that was good," November said. She was exhausted. She crawled up the steps, following her husband to their bedroom, where she collapsed onto their bed. As soon as they shut their eyes, the baby started to cry. She turned and looked at Tracy. He smiled and kissed her and went to see about his son. November was asleep before he made it to the door.

Chapter Eighteen

"'Love, love, love, love, love, love. Gimme that love,'" November sang with Jill Scott. She was feeling so good that she had pulled out Jill Scott's first CD and was listening to it in her truck. She and Tracy were in love, and they had been making love two or three times a day. She worked fewer hours at the office and made more love at home. Tracy was coming home in the middle of the day, hitting it, and going back to work. He would come in after work, and they'd get it in before dinner and again in the mornings before he left for work.

They were acting like sex-crazed teenagers, and November loved it. She got out of her Escalade and went into the mall to get some new lingerie. She had worked every number she had, and she wanted to keep it exciting. As she walked through the mall, she had that weird feeling again that someone was following her.

She stopped at a window and paid attention to the reflection in the glass to see if she was right. Then she saw a man watching her. She went inside of the store and pretended to look at clothes, and she tried to get a good look at him.

She tried to convince herself that it was just her imagination, but every move she made, his eyes were on her. She decided to get the hell outta the mall and call Tracy. She walked out to the parking lot and pulled out her phone. When he didn't answer, she didn't leave a message. She hit the end button and kept talking like she was in a conversation with someone. She opened the door and put her bags on the seat, and she was relieved that she made it inside of her truck safely.

When she put the key in to crank the truck, the man tapped on her window and scared the shit out of her. She tried to put the car in reverse, but he tapped the window again. If she backed out anyway, she may have run over his feet. She tried not to panic. He tapped the glass again and held up a pair of leather gloves. He waved them, and she realized they were hers. *How did he get those?* She relaxed a little and cracked the window.

"I'm sorry, ma'am, but you left these on the counter in Carson's," he said, trying to hand them to her. The window wasn't down far enough, so she hit the down button to open it a little more.

"I'm sorry, sir, but you shouldn't walk up on a woman in a parking lot. You scared me to death," she said, taking the gloves from him and letting up the window.

He tapped again. "I didn't mean to frighten you."

"Well, you did, and thank you for my gloves," she said trying to cut the conversation.

The man spoke again. "Listen, my name is Gordon, Kendell Gordon." He handed her a business card. "I'm in advertising, so if you have a business or know anyone who needs a slogan, please pass along my card."

"Is that right?" she asked, surprised to hear that they were in the same line of business. She relaxed a little.

"Yes, that's right," he said with a smile.

"Okay, that's my field. I work for Douglas & Knight."

"Oh, yeah, I've heard of them. I used to work for Gable, Harrison and White, but now I'm doing my own thing," he said, piquing her interest.

"I work there part-time now. I've been planning on going into business for myself too, but unfortunately, I haven't gotten the ball rolling."

"Why not? A pretty lady like yourself shouldn't have any problems getting business." He smiled at her.

"Well, I'm sure, but I don't think I'm ready to be on my own just yet," she said, giving an excuse. Truth was her husband didn't want her to go into business for herself.

"Well, whenever you think you are ready, let me know. Maybe I could be of help and pass on some pointers."

"Maybe," she said and smiled back.

"So, where are you going now? I was on my way to dinner," he said.

"Well, Mr. Gordon, as you can see, I am married." She held up the hand that was the home of her five-carat diamond and platinum wedding band. "And I have to get my son."

"I know you are married. That ring is blinding, trust me. I am not trying to hit on you, I promise. I was just inviting a pretty woman to share a meal. You may have some ideas that may be beneficial to me." He smiled his beautiful smile and November was flattered, but she only had eyes for Tracy.

"Well, Mr. Gordon, I would have to say no, because as a married woman I wouldn't accompany a man alone for dinner. But thanks for the invite. I have your card, and if there comes a time when I decide to get out there, and I need some advice, I'll be sure to use it. Here is one of my cards. Like I said, I work part-time at the agency. If you ever think about having a partner, let me know," she said. Maybe going into business with someone would be better. And maybe Tracy would let her start that way.

"Okay, Mrs. Stone," he said, examining her card. "You take care."

"You too," she said and backed out of the parking space.

She drove to her sister's house, smiling because she was happy with her life. She only wished she could start her own business. She couldn't understand why her husband didn't want to support her. She didn't want to keep getting chopped down by the old heads at the company she worked for who were so stuck in the Stone Age they often declined her edgy ideas. Being in business for herself would give her room to push her creativity to the max, and she dreamed of having that for herself constantly. She was content with her life and happy, but she desired more.

She got her baby and headed home. As usual, she put him down, changed, and got dinner on the stove. Tracy called and said he'd be late, so she didn't rush. She was sitting in the family room playing with TJ when her cell phone rang. She grabbed it from her bag. She didn't recognize the number.

"Hi, this is November," she said, not recognizing the number.

"November," a male said on the other end.

She didn't recognize the voice. "Yes?" she answered.

"Is this a bad time?"

"No, but who is this?"

"This is Kendell."

"Who?" she asked, confused.

"Kendell Gordon. You gave me your card earlier."

"Oh, Kendell," she said, wishing she'd never given him a card. She hadn't thought he'd be calling her that soon.

"Well, I wanted to know if I could interest you in a business proposition."

"What type of proposition?" she asked.

"Well, as I said earlier, I'm in business for myself, and I thought it would be wise to ask you to join me. You know, since you have experience. It may be an opportunity for you as well, to break out on your own too."

"That may be an avenue that I can take, but I'd have to first see your plans and proposals. And talk things over with my husband."

"Oh, so you have to have permission?"

"No, nothing like that, Mr. Gordon. My husband and I make business decisions together," she lied. Tracy did whatever he wanted to do whenever he wanted, and she never had a say when he wanted to start something new. "So I would have to run everything by him first."

"I understand that. How about we set up a meeting and I'll present you with my proposal? You can pass it on to your husband, and we can take it from there."

"Okay, that sounds good. When would you like to meet?"

"How about tomorrow for lunch?"

"Well, I don't think Tracy will be available. I'll have to let you know."

"Okay, I understand that, but my presentation is for you, Mrs. Stone. I'm not trying to go into business with your husband. Unless he does the same thing for a living and he is interested in going into business with me. I'm trying to have a business partner in the advertising field."

November took him to be a little cocky, but she liked his style. "Okay, I will give you a call in the morning after I check my schedule and we will go from there."

"Okay, Mrs. Stone. I look forward to hearing from you tomorrow."

"Okay, bye," she said and hung up. As soon as she put her phone back into her purse, Tracy walked in.

"Hey, baby," she said and walked over to greet him.

"Hey. How was your day?" he asked.

"Good and yours?

"It was long, and your man is starving," he said, walking over to the closet to hang up his coat. "Where's little man?"

"Over there in his playpen," she said, nodding toward the family room off the kitchen.

Tracy went over and picked him up, and they started playing. November wanted to say something about Mr. Gordon but decided not to. She wanted to wait until after she met with him before she told Tracy anything about it.

They ate dinner and November cleaned the kitchen while Tracy gave the baby a bath. She showered and couldn't wait to climb into bed with Tracy. She wanted him to give her a dose of his magic stick before they went to sleep. They made love, and she collapsed onto his chest. She smiled as she slid off him and lay next to him, trying to catch her breath.

She and Tracy were closer than they had ever been. She had gone from who she thought at one point in her life to be an ordinary, unlucky woman who God was punishing for some reason to a woman who had a loving husband, a healthy baby, and a beautiful home. How could a woman in her situation have anything to complain about? She was now more than content with her life, but she still longed for one thing.

She had everything she ever wanted but her own business. Why did her husband want her to settle for a part-time position working for a company that didn't allow her to reach her full potential? They held her back and didn't use her ideas or creative talent the way she felt they should. She was disgusted with working so hard for a slogan or a pitch, and they looked over her and went with someone else's idea.

She prayed and asked God for direction, and she closed her eyes. Then it came to her. If everything was legit with Mr. Gordon and she went into business with him for a couple of years, Tracy could see her abilities and would support her stepping out on her own. She could go in and have more responsibilities and show not only Mr. Gordon that she was brilliant, but prove to her husband that she had what it took to run a successful agency.

She was excited and couldn't wait to meet with Mr. Gordon to hear his plans for his new business and see if it was something she could actually be a part of. She not only hoped it was a good business opportunity, but she also hoped Tracy would be willing to support her on it. She said another silent prayer and asked God to pave the way for her and to allow her to be successful with her possible new prospect.

Chapter Nineteen

The next day, November met Kendell at his condo to pick up the proposal. She was kind of uncomfortable with the idea of meeting him there, but she went anyway. She got there at exactly twelve thirty, but he was still moving around doing other things.

"Would you like something to drink?" he asked, pouring himself a glass of iced tea.

"No, I have to be going. I have to meet my husband soon," she said, lying. She just didn't want to be at his place alone too long. It was not a good scene for a married woman to be at a man's condo in the middle of the day. Especially a man as fine as Kendell was. He was maybe five eleven and caramel complexioned with pair of hazel eyes that looked like honeycombs. He had a low-cut fade and a full beard and mustache that lay low and neat on his baby-smooth skin. He had on a pair of jeans and a nice button-down shirt, but that didn't camouflage his chiseled physique, and he was wearing a fragrance that November was familiar with, but she couldn't put her finger on the name.

He sat close to her at the center island to go over the papers, and the scent of his cologne drove her crazy. He smelled so damn good. She tried to avoid looking at him and making any eye contact because she didn't want to give him any ideas that she was interested in anything other than business. She wondered if he always dressed to impress and smelled good or if he had done it for her. He knew she was married and she thought she had made it clear that she wasn't interested in any extra attention from him, but with the way he was looking that afternoon, she wasn't sure he got it.

"I understand," she said, closing the folder. She stood to make her exit, but he struck up a new conversation.

"So, have you been to the mall lately?" he asked.

What? "No, not since yesterday." She gave him a weak smile. She just wanted to get out of there.

"Oh, I was just wondering. Do you shop at the mall all the time?"

"Yep, pretty much," she said, moving closer to the door. "Listen, Kendell, I really have to be going. Tracy, my husband, is expecting me soon."

"Okay," he said and walked her to the door. "Make sure you get back to me soon, okay? I'm anxious to know if we are going to be working together." He seemed professional in a way, but November felt that he was capable of doing some damage if she allowed him.

"I will let you know as soon as my husband and I make our decision."

"Well, I'm sure it will be fine. I look forward to hearing from you soon."

"Okay, take care," she said and walked out. She got to the elevator and was glad to be out of his space.

Now she had to figure out how she was going to present it to Tracy. She knew Kendell had a brilliant business plan and she knew it was a great opportunity, but would Tracy see it that way? She knew the main issue she would have to deal with was her working with a man. They had made huge progress, and Tracy was not tripping out on her. She had been enjoying her marriage and was afraid that this would send them back to square one.

She rode to April's thinking of every possible way to approach Tracy, but she came up with nothing. She thought about asking Kendell over to talk to him, but that wouldn't be a good idea either. She didn't want her husband to end up in

jail because he made a big deal about her innocently inviting a man over. She shook her head
and decided to stop thinking about ways to
approach Tracy with the idea of her quitting her
job to go out on her own. She was just going to
cook a nice meal, put the baby to bed, and present him with Kendell's business plans. He could
say either yes or no. Either way, she was leaving
Douglas & Knight.

She was going to have to figure out a way to
get around Tracy and make her dreams happen.
He had his businesses and did what he wanted
to do when it came to investments and starting
a new business. Why did he want to hold her
back and just make her a housewife? He knew
in the beginning, when they first started dating,
that she wanted to eventually open her very own
agency.

When she got home, she went ahead and fed
the baby and got him a bath and put him to bed.
She cooked Tracy's favorite meal, set the table
with the good china, and pulled out the candles.
She put on a nice satin and lace teddy set, put on
some soft music, poured some wine, and waited
for Tracy. Her hands trembled when she heard
the garage door open. She closed her eyes and
said a silent prayer, asking God to help her.

When Tracy walked in, he smiled. "Hey, baby, what's all this?" he asked, taking off his coat.

November walked over to him and took his coat and laid it on the bench by the door. "Nothing. I just wanted to have a romantic dinner with my man."

"Oh, so you just wanted a little QT with yo' man, huh?"

"Yes," she said and kissed him. "Come on, have a seat and let me get you a drink."

He sat at the table, and she poured him a glass of wine. She took his plate and loaded it with a rib eye, mashed potatoes, and green beans.

"And my favorite meal, too?" Tracy said, looking at his plate. "This is good."

He got up and went to the sink and washed and dried his hands then sat back in his place. He bowed his head and said grace and then he picked up his knife. November was so nervous she didn't say a word. She just took a few sips of her wine.

"So, Novey," Tracy said after he swallowed his first bite of food, "baby, what's really going on?"

"Huh?" She looked at him innocently.

"What's up? I know it's something. The candles are burning, the music is playing, and my son is not at the dinner table with us, so what's up?"

"Well, you know I've wanted to start my own business forever, right?"

He put his fork down.

"Come on, baby, just listen to me," she pleaded. "I know that you are not thrilled with that idea, but you know how bad I wanna leave Douglas and Knight."

"So quit. Stay home and take care of TJ."

"Baby, I don't want to just stay home. I wanna work. I want to have a career too."

"Novey, TJ isn't even seven months old yet. You have plenty of time to go back to work."

"Baby, I know, but you know how passionate I am. I've got so many ideas, and I am not growing at Douglas & Knight."

"November, I don't think this is a good time for you to be trying to get a business going. It takes a lot of work, and our son is so small. He needs his mother, Novey. I work long hours as it is, baby. The both of us don't need to be consumed by work, and I am tired of telling you that."

"Okay, Tracy, I get it. But you act like you don't care how I feel or what I want."

"Novey, I do care, but now is not the time."

"Okay then, since I'm not ready to go on my own, how about I go into a partnership with someone?"

"I don't know. I'd have to make sure that it's legit," he said and took a drink.

"Well . . ." she said, getting up and going over to the counter. She picked up the folder she had gotten from Kendell earlier and handed it to him.

"What's this?" he asked.

"A business proposal. I met this guy yesterday, and it turns out we are in the same field. He is starting his own business, and he wants me to go into business with him."

Tracy just looked at her. "You met some man? Where? When?" he yelled.

"Yesterday, Tracy." She gave him a short version of the story. "I was at the mall, and I left my gloves on the counter in a store. He ran after me and gave them to me. I thanked him, he gave me a card, and I gave him one of mine. He had heard of my company, and he also had heard about my work, so he asked if I was interested in being my own boss. We talked, and he presented me with an offer."

"Who is this cat, Novey?"

"His name is Kendell Gordon, and he is starting his own agency. He is looking for a fresh, motivated, creative agent to go into business with, so he asked me. I feel this is a good opportunity. I can work and do some of my own things, without a bunch of collars holding me back. This is a chance for me, Tracy."

He stood up and went to turn on the light. Then he sat back down, moved his plate, and opened the folder. November sat trying to keep from biting her manicured nails, nervous as hell. Tracy didn't say anything as he silently went over everything.

"Well," he finally said, "on paper, November, everything looks good, but I don't know. I need to check this cat out, babe."

"So I can do it, babe?" she said, getting excited.

"Hold on now, I'm not saying yes. I'm saying let me meet with this cat and talk to him and look him in the eye. I have a few questions, and I need to check out his background, get some references on his character, and a few other things. And then, maybe," he said.

November smiled. Maybe was good enough for her.

"November," he continued, "I love you, babe, and even though I don't think the time is right, I can see in your eyes how bad you want this. So, if this guy checks out . . ." He paused and looked at her. "Maybe, baby. Maybe."

"Maybe is good enough, Tracy. You just don't know how excited I am. I love you, baby, and I need your support."

"Listen, if this cat checks out and you take this on, you can't put us, our family, or our home on the back burner. I want a wife and a mother for my son. All this career and living out loud shit is cool for a single woman, not a married one. I'm not trying to hold you back, but you are my wife, and I need you to be here for us."

"I understand that Tracy, and I can do both. I just don't want to let my life pass me by without at least giving it a try."

"I know, babe. We'll see," he said, turning his attention back to his food.

November watched him eat, happy that he was at least going to consider it. She was ecstatic that he hadn't just said no. She knew in her heart that she would be able to work and take care of her family.

She knew she could do it.

Part Two

Chapter Twenty

"Listen, Trey, man," Kendell said, "I can't do this anymore. For one, it's not right. Two, you are taking this too far. Three, I've done everything but rape her, so face it, man, she isn't the one to cheat."

"No. This is not over. It hasn't been that long. I know she will break," Tracy said.

"Look, man, I'm tired and I'm done. I look like a desperate idiot who has no morals, no values or respect. If I make another pass at her, she is gonna quit, Tracy. And November is a creative woman. I don't want to lose her. Our business is doing well, and it is too important to the both of us to lose her now."

"I won't let her resign, Kendell. All I'm asking is for you to just take her out of town on this business trip and see if she gives. And if she doesn't, that is it. I will leave it alone, and I will back off. I just gotta know that my wife is not gon' let some man sweep her off her feet."

"Why, Tracy? Why can't you trust her and believe that she is a good woman? Tell me, why can't you relax, man, and accept that your wife is not Brianna? You need to realize that that was one woman, and that bullshit was so long ago."

"And what about Ana?"

"Man, you knew Ana was feeling Mike. She and Mike were off and on, on and off, so don't even try it. Now they are happily married, not thinking about your ass, and you are stuck in the past, miserable, letting what went down with those tricks interfere with your life. Come on, Trey, something else has to be bothering you, man. You have a son with this woman. November is a good woman, and you are playing with fire, man. Dude, let it go. This has gone too far."

"Oh, now you got a conscience? Back when you needed me to front you the dough to start your little business and get your company off the ground, it was all good. Now your shit is going well, and you wanna back out. I put up a lot of money for you, man. I put in your half and the half my wife brought to the table to make this dream of yours happen."

"I know, Trey, and I will pay you back every dime. Back then, yes, I did go along with it, but all it was supposed to be was a little flirting and to try to seduce her. I did, and she didn't go for it. Now you want me to take her out of town on some bogus business trip. That's taking it too far. Now that I've gotten to know her, she is an awesome woman who loves you to death, and everyone but you can see that. Even if I ask her to go out of town, she'll never go for that."

"You don't understand, Kendell. I love November, and I know she is a good woman. I just wanna be one hundred and ten percent sure. I just need to be absolutely sure."

"By what means, Trey? You are setting her up and trying to make her fall for another man. I have pulled every trick I can think of, and she won't give in. I'm telling you, if I cross the line again, she will resign. I will not let that happen. I am not doing this to her anymore."

Tracy's eyes narrowed. "You will do what you agreed you would do when I invested my money into your business. This isn't over 'til I say it's over, you got it?"

"Sorry, dawg, I'm done. And if you want to continue to do this to November, you go right ahead. She is a good woman. What man in his right mind would want to continue to play these games with his wife? I understood back then that you had some doubts and thought she was up to no good, and I understood your motive to want to put her to a test. But she didn't fail, and somehow, I think for your own sick pleasure, you wanted her to so you could prove your little theory. But guess what, Trey, not all woman cheat." Kendell got up to leave.

"Sit down!" Tracy demanded.

Kendell turned and looked at him. Tracy was obsessed. "Man, you have a problem."

"You think I have a problem?" Tracy asked. "Man, you don't know shit about me or what goes on in my life. You don't know me like that, and this is business. You gon' do what I tell you to do!" He stood up like he was challenging Kendell to walk out.

"I ain't doing shit, partner!" Kendell retorted, not backing down. He looked Tracy square in the eye. He wasn't interested in his games, and he didn't want to continue to do what he was doing to November.

"You're in love with her, aren't you?" Tracy asked. "That's the real reason you're backing out of our deal. It's written all over your mother-fucking face."

"Trey, you are crazier than I thought you were. You need to get some help and stop creating all of these delusions in your head."

"I'm not crazy, Kendell. I can see it in your eyes. You're in love with my wife."

"Whatever, man. I'm outta here."

Kendell walked out of Tracy's office. Why would Tracy say something like that? Yes, November was an exceptional woman. She was beautiful, intelligent, ambitious, and creative, and she had a great sense of humor. But above all things, she loved Tracy. Although he was an insecure, delusional idiot, she loved him.

Tracy had no idea what he had. November was faithful and true to him, and he wanted to turn her into a harlot. Kendell wished he had a woman that loyal to him in his life. He'd take care of her for sure and would never push some other man on her to prove a foolish point. If Tracy truly knew what he had, he'd stop the madness and appreciate it. He'd stop and thank God for sending him such an honest and dedicated woman.

In the beginning, when Kendell first agreed to do this, Tracy had him thinking that November was a scandalous, trifling adulteress he was trying to set up and catch in the act. After the first couple of weeks, however, Kendell started to see and realize that she was the exact opposite. She loved her family and her marriage, and she adored her son. All she talked about was her family, and she spoke highly of her husband. She always said how she was so proud of him for being such an honest, successful businessman.

At times, it made Kendell want to throw up when she spoke so highly of the man who paid him to seduce her. He wanted to just tell her, "Shut up. Your husband is slime, and the only reason you're here is because he paid me." He wanted so many times to just give her a hint or a heads-up, or send her an anonymous e-mail telling her the truth about the man she adored and respected so much, but at the same time, as he got to know her he didn't want to hurt her.

If Tracy made her happy the way she said he did, that was all Kendell wanted for her. He began to look at November for what she was, a good woman, and he knew she deserved better than Tracy. As much as he tried to fight it, he did start to have feelings for her. He got to a point where he avoided going into their office just to avoid her. He no longer wanted to go along with Tracy's plan, because it was useless anyway. November would always set him straight. The last time he went for the so-called gusto that Tracy had masterminded, she had threatened to resign if he ever crossed the line with her again.

Tracy didn't want to believe that it didn't work. Trying to kiss her on the lips after a late dinner they had with a client got him a slap across the face. She had made it clear that she wasn't going to tolerate his inappropriate behavior.

She threatened to file suit for sexual harassment after slapping the shit out of him. She also told him, "If you ever try that shit again, I will tell my husband." That made Kendell feel horrible, and he knew at that point there was no chance of him seducing her.

He regretted ever taking any money from Tracy, and he wished he would have never agreed to do what he did. None of it was worth it. He had grown to respect November, and he didn't want to continue to look her in the face and be a part of her husband's foolish schemes. He decided that he would give Tracy back his money by any means necessary to get him off his back. He knew that it was a stupid thing to do, but it was done, and he had to figure out something to fix it . . . without hurting November.

Chapter Twenty-one

"Hey, Kendell," November said when he picked up the phone. "Tracy told me you called me and said something about a business trip to New York."

Kendell was totally blown away that Tracy had proceeded to do what he had just told him earlier that day he wasn't going to do. "A trip to New York?" he asked, taken off guard.

"Yes. I just got in, and Tracy said you called earlier."

"Oh yes, the New York thing," he said, trying to think of something to say. "Well, that isn't set in stone yet, but there's a possibility that we may have to fly out to New York for a couple of days. I'm still trying to work out some details, but I don't know right now." He had no intention of going to New York. *Who in the hell does Tracy think he is?* he wondered, looking around his office for his cell phone. He was going to call him as soon as he was done talking to November.

"Who is it for?" November asked.

"Um, it's a potential client who is opening a new business in a few major cities. He may want us to handle his ads and slogans. He is swamped, and he may not be able to make it out here to Chicago so, like I said, I don't know right now."

"Okay, just keep me posted. I'm a mommy first, and I've got to talk to Tracy about it if I have to go out of town."

"I'm sure you do," he said sarcastically. She had to clear every second of her life with her crazy-ass husband, Kendell thought. "I will. Let me make a few calls, and I'll get back to you soon, okay?"

"Okay, bye," she said and hung up.

Kendell slammed the phone down and called Tracy immediately. "Man, what in the hell are you doing? I told you that I wasn't going out of town and I told you that I'm not going to be a part of your sick games."

"I am warning you, Kendell," Tracy said, "you will finish what you started, or your so-called business will be over. Done. I will fuck things up so bad for you, you'll be lucky to pump gas at Shell."

"Tracy, what are you trying to prove, man? You think you got so much pull in Chicago that I'm supposed to just do what the fuck you say?" Kendell asked. His grip tightened on the phone.

"Do you not hear what I'm saying, Kendell? You know who I know, and you know what the fuck I can do to you and your little agency, newbie. So don't try me, rookie."

"Tracy, man, listen. I am not trying to go there with you, man. I just want you to leave it alone. November doesn't deserve this. Man, she loves you."

"And I guess we'll see how much after this trip, won't we?"

"After this trip, Tracy, I'm done. I swear, after this trip, I'm done. I did what the fuck you asked me to do, and I'm telling you it doesn't matter if I take November to the moon. For some reason, she is hooked on you."

"Well then, we won't have anything to worry about, will we?"

"You're right, we won't." Kendell hung up the phone. He was so fucking mad that he threw his cell phone and broke it. He looked at the phone for a moment or two, wondering what the hell he'd agreed to. Then the phone on his desk rang out, jerking him back to reality, and he felt like shit.

"Kendell Gordon," he answered.

"Yeah, it's me, Trey. I will be sending a package with your itinerary. When you get it, you call Novey and tell her the flight info. When y'all get there, there's gonna be a mix-up with the reservation, and you're gonna end up having one room."

"Trey, man, November is never gonna go for that."

"Don't worry about her. Just don't let her make another reservation. You make her think that you're gonna call around and get another room. Let me handle November."

"Then what?" Kendell asked.

"Then you romance her. I know you know how to do that, Casanova." Tracy laughed.

"Tracy, for the record, if your marriage goes to shit, keep in mind that it was you, not her."

"Let me worry about that. I'll be in touch." Tracy hung up.

Kendell got up and went over and picked up his broken cell phone. Taking a break, he left the office to buy a replacement. When he got back, the package was on his desk. He figured the receptionist had left it there for him before she left for the day.

Inside the package, he found a flight itinerary, the hotel confirmation, and $3,000 in cash. Tracy pulled out all the stops for Kendell to show November a good time, and that was exactly what he planned to do. He secretly hoped November would give in so she could be his and Tracy would leave her and get the hell out of the picture.

Kendell sat down and dialed November. She didn't pick up her cell phone, so he dialed her house. Tracy picked up: the last person he wanted to talk to.

"Tracy, this is Kendell," he said.

"Oh, hey, Kendell. What's up, man? How are things?" he asked like they were the best of friends.

"I'm fine, Tracy. Where is November?"

"Oh, she's right here. Hold on, I'll put her on."

November's soft, sweet voice came on the line. "Hey, Kendell. How are you?"

"I've had better days," he said and took a deep breath. "Um, listen, we are gonna have to go out to New York after all. This client is mad busy, so he agreed to pay for our flight, hotel, meals, et cetera. Are you up for a trip?"

"Not really, but if you really need me to go, I guess I have to, huh?"

"Actually, the client is requesting you. He says that you come highly recommended."

"Oh, really?" November said. "This could be just what our company needs to compete with the heavy hitters."

"Yes, ma'am. So, you're going?"

"Of course. I just need to run this by Tracy, which won't be a problem, because I told him earlier that there was a chance and he was okay with it."

I'll bet he was. "Well, we are scheduled to leave tomorrow. He'll let us know when he can fit us into his schedule when we get there."

"What type of company is it? So I can prepare."

"Cosmetics is all I know for now. This client is so big he only wants to deal face-to-face." It killed him to keep on lying to her.

"Okay then, what time tomorrow?"

"Early. Our flight leaves at eight a.m." he said, reading from the itinerary.

"Okay. I'll have Tracy bring me to the airport."

"Well, I can pick you up if you like," he offered.

"That's up to you."

"I'm just saying, so he doesn't have to drag your son out that early. We have to be there two hours before departure."

"Okay. Well then, I'll see you in the morning," she said. "Oh, Kendell, for how long?"

"Well, the reservations are for three days."

"Three days? Damn."

"I know, right?"

"Well, I guess that's just the way it is. I sure hope this client is worth it," she said.

Kendell wanted to say, "Nope. He's your typical asshole," but he resisted.

Chapter Twenty-two

November hated to kiss her son good-bye the morning she left for New York, and she had to drag herself away from her husband's embrace. Kendell picking her up was a good idea because she didn't want to get TJ up that early. She rubbed his sleeping face for the final time and headed for the door. Tracy had loaded her bags into Kendell's Lexus.

"I'm gonna miss you guys," November said, giving Tracy another soft kiss and a tight hug.

"I'm gonna miss you too," he said, giving her a warm smile.

"Are you sure you guys will be okay?"

"Yes. I can handle my son for a few days, Novey," he assured her. "Stop worrying."

"I know, but I've never left him for days before, Tracy. What if—"

Tracy cut her off. "Shhh," he said, putting his finger over her lips gently. "We will be fine. If I need help, I'll call your sister. She's a baby professional," he joked.

November smiled. "Okay, okay. I'm just gon' miss you guys."

"And we are gonna miss you. Now go before you miss your flight," he said, opening the car door. "Now, Kendell, you take care of my wife. I don't wanna have to kill you." He winked at Kendell.

Yeah, you want me to take care of her all right. "I gotcha, Trey," he said.

"I love you, baby," Tracy said, giving November a final kiss.

"I love you too, Tracy," she said.

Kendell looked away to avoid watching them interact with each other. He felt like slapping the shit out of Tracy's phony ass.

"Bye," he said to Tracy and shut the door.

Kendell pulled out of the driveway and headed for the airport. The ride was kind of quiet, not too much conversation. After they checked in, they sat in silence, waiting to board. November pulled out her cell phone and dialed home. Tracy picked up on the third ring, and from the sound of his voice, she could tell that he had gone back to bed, so she didn't keep him long.

The flight was horrible. November was not used to flying, so she got airsick and threw up all of her meal from the night before. When they got to the hotel, she was more disappointed to find out that their so-called client had reserved only one room and the hotel was booked to capacity.

"You've got to be kidding me," she said to the clerk.

"I'm so sorry, ma'am. I'm afraid we are totally booked, but your room is a suite with a pull-out sofa bed, and there is plenty of room for two," the nice clerk explained.

November turned to Kendell. "No way can I stay in the same room with you." Tracy would drop dead if she told him that. She turned back to the desk clerk. "I understand, but I am a married woman, and I can't stay in the same room with him," she said, pointing at Kendell.

"I know, but there is nothing available. I can put you on the waiting list, and I can call around for you."

"Please, because I need my own room. I don't care how much it is, just please find me a room."

"I will, ma'am. Just go up, and I will call your room when I have something."

"Please. Thank you so much," she said.

When they got on their floor, November was impressed. The hotel was beautiful. When she walked into their suite, she was more impressed. It was huge, and it had everything. The tub was so big she could swim in it.

"Listen, November, I can get another room. This is a room fit for a queen, and you should stay here."

"No, that's okay, Kendell. Trust me, I wouldn't mind you sleeping on the couch, but I know Tracy would have a heart attack if he knew we only had one room."

"I know, but I don't mind finding another room."

"Are you sure? I don't want to put you out. I mean, this room is a gorgeous room and I don't want to deprive you either."

"It's cool. If she finds another room, I'll go. If not, I will have to sleep out here tonight and get something tomorrow."

"Okay, but hopefully she calls with some good news because I can't lie to Tracy."

"Don't lie. Just don't say anything."

"I don't know, Kendell."

"Look, handle it however you want. I'm gonna run downstairs and check out the lounge and have a drink. Do you wanna come?"

"In a few. I wanna call home first. I know I talked to Tracy when we landed, but I told him I'd call when we got checked in."

"Okay, I'll be in the lounge. Are you feeling better?"

"Yes, much better," she said. He turned to walk away, and she called to him, "Hey, Kendell."

He stopped.

"Thank you for everything. I know if it had been the other way around, and you were blowing chunks on the plane, I may have acted as if I didn't know you." She giggled.

"No problem." He smiled and left.

"Look, man, I told you she wasn't gonna go for it," Kendell told Tracy. "She is freaking out, and she doesn't deserve to be under this type of stress, man. This is crazy. She's got the clerk looking for another room." He had called Tracy as soon as he got down to the lobby.

"What? She's not going for the sofa bed deal?"

"Hell, naw. She keeps going on and on about not being able to stay in the same room with me and how she isn't comfortable with it, man. I told you that this would never work."

"It's okay. I will call and talk to her. You just stay downstairs and wait for her." Tracy hung up. He called November's cell phone.

She answered on the second ring. "Hey, baby. I'm so happy you called."

"Hey, my love. I see I missed your call a few minutes ago. I was changing TJ. Are you feeling better?"

"Yes. I mean, I was until we got to this hotel. This asshole of a client only booked one room."

"What?" he said, sounding surprised.

"Yes, and the hotel is freaking sold out."

"How big is the room?"

"It's an enormous suite. And it's beautiful. I mean, this guy spent a pretty penny, but he could have saved his money and gotten two regular rooms."

"So why are you stressing? It's a suite, my love."

"Because it only has one bed, Tracy. Are you on crack? There's a let-out couch in the other room, but I want a room by myself."

"I know, but Kendell is a standup guy, and I'm sure he'd take the sofa." November was silent. "Are you there, Novey?"

"Yes, I'm here, but are you? Who are you and what have you done with my husband? You've gotta be an imposter. You mean to tell me that you would be okay with Kendell staying in the same room with me?"

"No, but I'm sure you know how to conduct yourself. It's only three days, babe."

"Tracy, are you high?" she asked.

"No." He chuckled a bit. "No, I'm not high, baby. I'm fine. You just need to not worry and do your job and get back home."

"Are you sure? Because the clerk is looking to find me another room somewhere else since they are all booked up here."

"Yes, I'm sure. I'd feel better if you were safe in the Big Apple, and if you are with Kendell, I'll feel better than if you were in another hotel somewhere else in a strange city alone. That would make me more nervous than Kendell crashing on the couch."

"Well, you have a point. I don't know anything about this city. I'll just see if they have something for tomorrow in this hotel so I can move to another room."

"That sounds good. Just relax, baby, I'm good. I want you safe, and I trust you."

"Okay, my love. I'm glad you called, because I was freaking out."

"No need. Now, let me get back to our son and get him some lunch."

"Okay. Kiss him for me and tell him that Mommy loves him very much."

"What about his daddy?"

"Aww, you know I love you, big daddy," she said, smiling. "I'm gonna meet Kendell downstairs. I will call you later, okay?"

"Okay, baby. Later," he said, and they hung up.

Chapter Twenty-three

Tracy was scared that he may have pushed too much, but it was done. This was November's final test. If she passed, he could relax and live worry free.

As soon as he hung up with November, he dialed Kendell.

"This is Kendell," the other man answered.

"Okay, Kendell, it's all good. She is going to stay. And this time, you'd better do exactly what I told you to do, because I know what Novey likes and I know what a man has to do to sweep her off her feet."

"Yeah? Just like you did?" Kendell said sarcastically.

"Look, Kendell, you don't understand, so enough with the sarcasm. I love my wife more than you'll ever know. I just need to prove that, if given the right opportunity or the perfect chance, she will forget all about me and do what she will."

"And if you are wrong?" Kendell asked.

"Then I can move on with my marriage, with no doubts."

"I hope this gives you what you need, because any man in his right mind would not go to this extreme. If you have all these doubts, why did you marry her?"

"Because I fell in love with her. I honestly love my wife."

"Whatever. I can't wait until this bullshit is all over."

"You just concentrate on our deal and stick to the program—"

"Gotcha," Kendell said, cutting him off. "Look, November is coming, so I gotta go." He hung up.

Tracy tossed his phone and prayed that November was the woman she'd vowed to be. It would kill him if she went there with Kendell.

November went to sit at the bar with Kendell. "So, have you talked to this mysterious client yet?" she asked.

"Nope, not yet. Just waiting to hear back from his assistant."

"Okay. Well, I talked with Tracy, and he is okay with you staying in the room with me tonight. But tomorrow, I'm still gon' try to get another room."

"That's cool. What do you want to drink?"

"Hell, let me see. Are we going to be meeting with our client today?"

"Probably not. I don't think he will be seeing us today. His assistant said sometime tomorrow."

"Okay then. I'll take a Long Island Iced Tea," she said.

"All righty then," he said and ordered.

They sat hours and talked and laughed and drank. It was after six when they decided to get a cab and go to dinner. They ate and talked some more, and he enjoyed her company. When they made it back to their suite, November insisted Kendell use the shower first, because she wanted to call home again.

Kendell came out to find November on the terrace. It was cold, so he grabbed his coat then two mini bottles of chilled wine from the wet bar. He went out and handed one to her.

"Pretty cold to be out here tonight."

She took the bottle. "Thanks, Kendell. It is, but this place is amazing. I wish Tracy were here to see this."

Kendell's mood shifted. He did not want to talk about Tracy. He wanted to just hear about her. He wanted to talk to November without hearing a laundry list of great things about Tracy. He was the bad guy, and if November knew better, she'd leave his crazy ass.

"Yes, I guess it would be nice to be out here with your man," he said drily.

"Oh, I'm sorry, Kendell. I know I talk about Tracy a lot, but you have to understand that he is my husband and the first man I fell in love with."

"So you mean to tell me that he is that good?"

"What do you mean?"

"I mean, when I'm around him, he seems so insecure. Like he is just waiting for me to cross the line so he can behead me or something."

She giggled. "Tracy is just like that. He's been like that for the longest, but trust me, he has gotten one hundred and ten percent better. He just thinks every guy wants me—or, I should say, he used to think that." She moved from the railing and sat down.

"Well, if you were my wife, I'd think the same thing," he said.

She smiled. "Well, Tracy used to be that way. But I guess now he realizes that it doesn't matter what a man says or does; it's how I respond. And he knows now that I love him and want only him."

"Yeah, I guess," he said and walked over to the railing.

"So, Mr. Gordon, where is your special lady?"

"I don't have one of those," he said and took a sip.

"Why not? You are successful and a good catch."

"I have lady friends, or girlfriends, whatever you wanna call it." He shrugged. "I'm just not with the one I want. There are opportunities, but I'm looking for a certain type."

"Well, keep in mind there are no perfect women out there."

He turned to face her. "I know. I'm not looking for perfection, just a woman on a certain level with certain qualities."

"Yes, I can understand that. I didn't think Tracy would be interested in me when we first met, or even fall for someone like me, but he did." She sipped her wine.

"What do you mean, November? You're a beautiful woman."

"Man, please. I am decent, though."

"What's wrong with you? What makes you think you're just decent?"

"For one, my husband is handsome and fit and has the body of a god. I was a plain Jane when we met. You know, no glam and the thick sista, as they say, and the women who used to hang around Tracy were like drop-dead gorgeous. To be honest, I was a bit insecure, but after we started dating and hanging out, my confidence was boosted, and I stepped up my game. Not because I thought someone would take him, but I wanted to look like I was with him," she explained. "Like you. You are very attractive, and I see how women respond to you, so if I were your woman, I wouldn't just let myself go. I feel the same way with Tracy."

"I know what you mean, but to me, you are a gorgeous woman, and in my opinion, Tracy needs to step up his game to hold on to you. My question after meeting Tracy was, 'How in the hell did he get her?'"

"Whatever. That's what you say now, but if I were single and available, a guy like you wouldn't give me the time of day. Or, if you would have met me back then, you probably wouldn't have noticed me." She took another sip.

"Nope, that is where you are wrong," he said. "You don't recall me making passes at you when we first met? How you slapped the shit outta me for trying to kiss you?"

She laughed. "Yes, I remember. But that's because I carry myself like the woman I want people to see me as, and I slapped you because you crossed some serious lines. If I had told Tracy, you'd be out here in the NY by yo'self." They laughed.

"Yes, I was outta line, but for the record, Mrs. Stone, you are my type. I honestly can't see you being less beautiful than you are now. Your husband has no idea what he has."

"Oh, he knows." She winked. She sipped her drink and turned to gaze out at the city.

No, the hell he doesn't, Kendell thought.

They were quiet for a few brief moments, and then he went for more wine. This time, he brought bac a bottle and two glasses.

"Here you go," he said, handing her a glass, when he came back.

"Thanks. I was wondering what was keeping you, but it's so gorgeous I couldn't bring myself to go and check."

"Yes, I decided to get a bottle." He sipped and then sat. "So, you wanna check out New York? It's still early."

"Sure, just let me shower and change," she said.

While she showered, Kendell got dressed, hating that he wanted Tracy's wife. The thought of her in the bathroom naked gave him an erection. He fantasized about holding her and making her insides sing. He wanted to feel her skin on his skin.

He shook it off and tried to focus on something else. When she came out to the living room area ready to go, he was speechless. She had on a pair of sexy jeans that framed her hips and ass perfectly, a low-cut sweater, and a pair of red high-heeled boots. She looked damn good.

"You ready to see New York?" he asked.

"I sure am." She smiled brightly, and he wanted to kiss her right then and there.

"Then let's do this," he said.

When they got back, it was after two a.m. November was definitely wasted. She was singing and laughing at her own jokes, and she had Kendell cracking up. In the cab on the way back to the hotel, she had rested her head on his shoulder. When they got into the elevator, he had to help her stand up.

It wasn't that she drank too much; it was that the two she'd had at the jazz club they went to were strong. She'd only had one weak-ass drink in the hotel lounge—that's how she described it, saying, "this watered-down mess"—and wine in the room. And she hadn't finished her refill.

When they got inside the room, she kept talking and talking, and Kendell tried to get her to shut up. It was cute and all, but she wasn't making any sense. She told him about when she and her sister, April, were growing up and how everybody used to tease them about their names. He laughed hard when she said that April used to make the other kids think she was a witch and would threaten to cast a spell on them if they didn't leave them alone. She told him that most of the kids were scared of April because they really believed that she had some type of powers. She told story after story until he helped her to bed.

He could have easily taken advantage of her the way her husband wanted him to, but he couldn't.

Kendell removed November's boots and put her to bed in her clothes. He stroked her cheek and brushed her bangs to the side and stood there for a few moments and looked at her face. He couldn't resist giving her a soft kiss. Tons of malicious thoughts ran through his mind as he caressed her skin, but he cared for her too much to cross the line. He did give her one more soft kiss before he turned out the light and closed the bedroom door.

He went to the sofa but didn't bother to pull out the bed. Instead, he grabbed the remote and tried to watch a bit of TV. He couldn't concentrate, however, because he wanted too badly to go back into the room with November and just lie next to her and hold her. He rubbed a hand across his erection and tried to put her out of his mind. Finally, he got up and went for the extra blanket and pillow and forced himself to fall asleep.

Chapter Twenty-four

The next morning, the aroma of hotcakes and sausage woke November up. At first, she thought she may have been dreaming. She struggled to open her eyelids, and once she could focus, she saw the cart with silver dome lids covering mouthwatering platters of food.

"Good morning," she heard Kendell say from the doorway.

She sat up. "What's all this?"

"Breakfast," he said.

"You didn't have to do that, Kendell."

"I know, but I did it anyway. So get up and come and put something in your tummy. Our client has arranged for us to enjoy some festivities today."

"What? How are we here on business and no business has taken place?"

"Well, Mrs. Stone, I met with Mr. Reed early this morning, and it seems he is going to allow us to work on his new account and get back to him with some ideas. Since the meeting was so brief, he offered us a car for the day and wrote out a nice check for us to see New York."

"So that's it? We flew all the way out here for one brief meeting that I didn't get to attend? I mean, I didn't have to come." She frowned.

"I guess I was just as surprised as you are."

"I'm not surprised, Kendell. I'm upset. I mean, I've never been to New York before, but to leave my baby for three days is a little upsetting."

"I know, November, and I know how hard it was for you to leave your son for these couple of days, but think of it as a little vacation." He smiled.

November didn't smile. "Well, Kendell, I didn't need a vacation from my family." She got up from the bed and walked into the bathroom.

After taking off her clothes and putting on the complimentary robe that was hanging near the shower, she used the toilet and brushed her teeth. She stared into the mirror, frustrated and pissed off that she had agreed to come along on the stupid trip. *Kendell could have taken care of this by himself,* she thought as she dried her hands.

When she shut off the water, she heard tapping on the door.

"November, I could call to get an earlier flight if you'd like," Kendell offered. "I hate that you're upset and I feel awful for dragging you out here for nothing. I know being away from your baby is hard, and I'm sorry."

She opened the door. "No, it's okay. It's not your fault, and I'm not trying to take my frustrations out on you. I just have never been away from my baby overnight," she said, coming out of the bathroom. "But to be perfectly honest, I haven't slept that good in months." She sat at the table to eat. "Wow, this is good. Did you eat already?"

"Yeah," he answered. He sat in the chair across from her. "So you slept well? You look radiant, like you got a great night of sleep. I mean, your skin is flawless, almost like you're glowing."

"I woke up like this," she teased with a smile. He chuckled. "Seriously, I did. That big bed to myself, without Tracy scratching me with his toenails, was nice," she joked.

"Well, you will have one more peaceful, scratch-less night."

"I wonder how Tracy slept without me," she said, going for her phone. She tried home first, but there was no answer. Then she dialed his cell, and when it went straight to voice mail, she decided to try him later. "Well, I guess my guys are doing just fine without me."

"Or maybe you should relax. Come on, November, we both know you are a dedicated mother and wife. Just take today and do you," Kendell suggested.

"Do me? I haven't done me in so long I've forgotten how to just do me."

"Well, today we are gonna jolt your memory. If you wanna shop, then shop. If you wanna sleep, then sleep. Watch TV all day and order room service, be my guest."

"Yeah, that's not a bad idea. I hardly ever get me time. It will be good just to do what I wanna do, and not just what I have to do."

"See? Now, tell me, what do you want to do?"

"Well, I've always wanted to go to Central Park. I used to watch *Sex and the City* faithfully, and it was like Manhattan was the place to be."

"Well, get dressed and let's see Manhattan."

"Okay, but let me try Tracy one more time." She wanted to see how the baby was doing.

"Okay," Kendell said and went into the other room of the suite.

She dialed Tracy again and still got no answer. She left him a message and figured he'd call her when he got up.

After she showered and dressed, November and Kendell left to explore the city. They shopped, ate well, and hit every tourist attraction they could. By the time they got back to their suite,

November was tired, and her body was aching. She peeled off her boots and sat on the sofa for a moment.

"I have a surprise for you," Kendell said, coming into the room where she was.

"Oh, really?" she asked curiously.

"Yes. You just go in there and take your shower, and you'll get it after you come out."

November smiled. She'd had such a great time with Kendell, and she was sure his surprise would be something good. She got up and tried calling Tracy again. She hadn't heard from him the entire day, and that was unusual. When he didn't answer again, she focused on not worrying. She figured if something had happened, April or someone would have called her.

After showering, putting on a set of comfortable cotton pajamas, brushing her teeth, and washing her face, she left the bathroom. She couldn't wait to see the surprise Kendell had for her.

"Aww. Ooh, ooh. Yes, that feels good," November moaned. The sounds of jazz carried softly through the candlelit room. She closed her eyes and sighed.

"You like that?" Kendell asked softly.

"Oh, yes," she moaned.

"I told you that this would help you feel better."

"Aww, yes, indeed. If only I could get this every day at home."

"I'm glad you like it."

"Aww, yes. Lower," she insisted. "Ooh, harder. Yeah. Yeah, oooh, yes, like that. That's perfect," she moaned. She didn't want to move. She wanted it to last forever.

"Just relax, November," he whispered.

"I am. This is just too good," she said breathing deeply.

"I knew you'd love it."

"Yes, yes. Yes, I do. Ooh, Kendell, it does feel good."

Just then, Tracy burst through the adjoining door. "Motherfucker!" he yelled.

Kendell and November jumped in surprise.

Chapter Twenty-five

Earlier That Day

On Tracy's flight to New York, he kept telling himself that November was a good woman and he'd surprise her instead of allowing her the opportunity to give Kendell her body. When he got there and they were out, he was disappointed. He waited in the lobby for a couple hours, trying to surprise her, but they never showed.

He didn't want to go up to his room that was adjoined to their room, because he wanted to see her when she came into the lobby, but he finally just decided to go up and wait for her. He went to the desk and verified that his company had set up the reservations and that the direct billing was going to his credit card for the room, and the clerk gave him a key to both rooms.

He went into their room first and snooped a bit then unlocked the adjoining door. He hurried out of their room and went into his suite to listen for them to come in. After about thirty minutes, he heard Kendell and November talking and laughing, but he could barely make out what they were saying. He stood posted to the door and heard another voice, but the words didn't come through clear enough.

He heard a little bumping and thumping, but since he couldn't see what was going on, the suspense drove him insane. Shortly after that, all he heard was soft music and the moaning sounds November made with him. His hands began to shake.

Tracy couldn't bear to listen another moment. He had had enough. He couldn't believe what he was hearing. He was so hurt, more hurt than he had imagined he would be. He wished he had never ever set any of this up. He knew he had pushed too hard and had gone too far. Now, the woman he loved was loving another man. The woman he hoped would never give in to Kendell had finally given in to him.

He tried to hold back tears, but it was impossible. He wished he could take it all back. He wished he had stayed in Chicago and just waited for her to come home. That way, he would have never known. Maybe Kendell would have lied and covered up their affair. Hurt gave way to outrage. He hated Kendell for actually touching his wife. He hated himself even more for instigating it. He wanted to kill Kendell.

"You motherfucker!" he yelled, breathing hard.

The room's inhabitants jumped in surprise. Kendell turned around from the chair he was sitting in, and November's head popped out of the hole of the massage table she was lying on. The masseur jumped and almost knocked over his little table of oils.

"Tracy!" November yelled.

Kendell looked at him with no words. He just shook his head.

"What's going on, Tracy?" November asked. "What are you doing here?" She got off the table holding the wrap in place that she had around her body.

Tracy stood there confused, but he was relieved that the unthinkable was not going on. He was so embarrassed he didn't know what to say.

"Tracy, baby, when did you get here? Please tell me what is going on," November demanded.

"It's over, man. It's over!" Kendell yelled and walked out.

"What's over, Tracy? What? Please say something. Tell me what in the hell is going on."

The masseur packed his equipment and left quickly.

Tracy stood frozen, too dumbfounded to speak. He had been so wrong about November.

"Baby, say something. What in the hell is going on, Tracy?"

"I'm sorry, Novey. I love you, and I'm sorry." He turned and walked out.

November didn't have a clue what had just happened. She ran after him, but he took the stairs. She couldn't go down without clothes on, so she went back into the room and dressed as quickly as she could. By the time she got down to the lobby, he was nowhere to be found. She dialed his phone repeatedly, but she couldn't get him. She tried Kendell, but he wouldn't pick up either. She roamed the lobby hoping to find one of them, but she didn't. They weren't out front either.

She had no clue where to begin to look for either of them. She went back up to the room and called Tracy, dialing his number back to back and leaving a ton of messages. She tried calling Kendell, but he still didn't pick up either.

It's over. It's over, was the only thought running through her mind. She sat on the couch and turned on the TV. She tried Tracy again, but nothing, so she went to the wet bar for a drink to ease her mind. Sipping, she paced the floor.

After about an hour, she heard the door. She ran to it, thinking it was Tracy, but when it opened, it was Kendell.

"Kendell, what happened? Have you seen Tracy?" she asked. He didn't answer her. "Kendell, please, I have to know what's going on." She grabbed his arm.

"You don't wanna know what's going on, November. You are so in love and so blinded by what you feel. Trust me, you don't wanna know the truth."

"What, Kendell? What are you talking about? I don't understand."

"It's a lie. Everything was a lie, and your sorry-ass husband is too scared to face you and tell you the truth. Instead, he wants to blame me for his sick, twisted schemes. I'm done with you, and I'm done with him. I'm done with this shit. How I fell into this bullshit is beyond me, but I'm done with it, that's for damn sure. You go back to your perfect life with your wonderful husband and your fairytale life, like everything is perfect. Best of luck to you."

"Kendell, I don't know what this is about. Where is Tracy? What is a lie? You're not making any sense. What schemes? Tell me what you're talking about."

"Your crazy-ass husband is downstairs in the lounge. He would rather blame everybody else for his problems instead of owning up to them. So go downstairs and ask your perfect husband what's going on. Better yet, I'll send him up on my way out, because I'm sure he wants another opportunity to swing on me." He grabbed his garment bag out of the closet and went into the bathroom.

November followed him, asking question after question, but he ignored her. "Kendell, please. I . . . I need to know. Please tell me."

"November, you are a good person, and you deserve so much more. All I can say is you have to see him for who he is. If he loved you, he'd get some help and stop obsessing over you cheating."

"What? That's what this is about?" she said in a panic. "Tracy thinks we are messing around? He thinks we are having an affair? I'll talk to him, Kendell. I can clear this up!"

"No!" he yelled. He paused for a moment. "I'm sorry for yelling. You're the victim. You fell in love with the wrong man, and that's not your fault. Listen, November, you've got to get him some help if you love him. If you knew the truth about it all . . ." He paused. "I care for you too much to hurt you. The truth needs to come from him, not me."

"You tell me the entire truth. Tell me what Tracy said to you."

"Talk to your husband, November," he said.

She didn't fight him anymore. She grabbed her purse and headed for the door. She turned to him before walking out. "Kendell, please don't leave. Please. I don't know what's going on, but I have a feeling I may need a friend when I'm done."

He looked at her for a moment without speaking. Finally, he said, "Okay."

November went downstairs to the lounge, but Tracy was nowhere to be found. She sat down and tried to hold back the tears. What did Tracy do? What did he do to her? Why did he pretend to be happy and okay with her going to New York when he wasn't? Why did he act like he was so cool with her and Kendell staying in the same room if he thought they were having an affair?

Her cell phone rang. It was Tracy.

"Tracy, thank God. Where are you, baby?"

"Look, I messed up, and I don't know if you'll ever forgive me."

"Tracy, what is it? Please tell me. Whatever it is, we can work it out."

"I wish that were true, my love, but it's not."

"Trey, where are you? Let's talk, baby. I'm your wife. Tell me where you are so I can come and we can talk."

"Listen, after Kendell tells you the truth—and I know he will—you will never forgive me, so I will stay away for a while and let you decide what you want to do. Just know that I am so sorry, for everything. I have to get my head together and do what everybody has told me, even you, over and over again. I gotta get some help. I love you, Novey. Take care of my son for me. I'm sorry."

November became angrier. All she wanted was answers, but he refused to give her that. "No, Tracy, you need to tell me what the hell happened. You think I'm having an affair with Kendell. You came out here to try to catch me with Kendell, and then you run out on me. I haven't done anything, Tracy. Why are you treating me this way? I am not messing with Kendell, so why won't you talk to me?"

"I know you're not, November. Dammit! November, I know. It isn't you. It's me. I needed so badly to trust you. I tried so hard to trust you, but I just couldn't. What I did to you is unforgivable. You didn't deserve what I did. You didn't do anything wrong, baby. It's not you. I love you, Novey, but I have a problem, and I've got to do this on my own."

"Please, Tracy," she cried. She wanted to see him. She wanted to know the truth. She wanted to know what in the hell he was talking about.

"Novey, I love you and TJ. I'll be in touch." He ended the call.

November called him right back, dialing him again and again, but he didn't answer. Somehow, she managed to make her way back upstairs without breaking down completely. When she opened the door, Kendell was still there, just like he said he would be.

Kendell had contemplated whether he should leave. He didn't want to just bail because, after she talked to Tracy, he was sure she was going to need him. Plus, he was guilty too, so he knew he'd have to face the music. He knew she was going to be mad at him too but oh, well. He fixed a stiff drink, sat down on the sofa, and waited for her to return.

When she walked in, her face was drenched with tears. She went over to him and cried in his arms. After a few moments of sobbing, she went into the bathroom. She came back and sat down with him, and her eyes started watering again.

"Don't cry, November. I don't want to see you cry."

"I just don't know what I did. I tried to be a good wife. I tried to be," she said, sobbing again. "He said you would tell me the truth. What is he talking about, Kendell? Please, somebody needs to tell me something."

"November, don't. Please." He reached for one of her hands and held it.

"Kendell, what did he do? How does this involve you?"

"November, you don't want to know."

"Yes, I do. If Tracy won't tell me and you know something, you need to tell me."

Kendell sighed and released her hand. "November, first I want to tell you that I am sorry. It started out only to prove a point, but I . . . I went with it like a jackass, and I'm so sorry. I knew I should have said no in the first place." He told her the entire story. He even told her that, in the process, he fell for her. He didn't leave anything out.

November jumped to her feet. "So, you mean to tell me my husband went through all of this just so you could get me in bed? He put you up to wine and dine me, in hopes I'd forget about my vows to him and give you some pussy? He basically pimped me out to you!" she yelled.

"Well, that was the plan, but I swear to you that I didn't want things to go down like that. You gotta believe me. I tried so many times to call it off, I promise. I wasn't trying to get you in bed. I honestly thought you were someone else in the beginning, but after seeing that you were not the woman Tracy described, I didn't want to do it anymore. But it was too late. I had already taken the money and Tracy wouldn't ease up."

"Oh," she spat, "you care about me so much, but you couldn't tell me what was going on, Kendell?"

"I didn't wanna see you hurt, November. I didn't want to hurt you."

"Whatever, Kendell. You're no better than Tracy. You're not a saint or innocent."

"November, stop it, okay? I know I was wrong, and I'm not making any excuses for myself. I was stupid to go along with it, but I never wanted things to go this far. I didn't want it to happen this way. I wanted to go home tomorrow and tell Tracy that nothing happened and let that be the end of this charade. I had no idea Tracy was coming to New York. We never talked about him coming here."

"You're no different," she cried.

"Please, November, don't cry. I'm sorry. I wish I could take it all back. I wish I would have told you the truth a long time ago."

"But you didn't. I don't trust you, and I don't want to ever see you again."

"Come on, November, don't say that. I will never cross any lines with you. I want you to be happy, and if that is with Tracy, I want that for you. I never tried to sleep with you, and you know that. I thought that once I came on this trip, we would go home and everything would be normal. As much as I care about you, November, and want to have you for myself, I didn't go there with you because I respect you. We work well together, and I don't want to stop working with you."

"You don't actually think we can just go back to normal, Kendell, do you? I mean, seriously?"

"We can try, November. Please. If you leave right now, I don't know what I'll do without you. You are brilliant, and we both know you love your work. Don't leave. Take as much time as you want, just don't leave."

"I'm sorry, Kendell, but like you said, it's over. I don't think I can work with someone like you."

"November, please. November."

She turned away from him.

"That's it?" he asked.

"Bye, Kendell. I will send for my things when I get back to Chicago."

"November, please. I know you are upset right now, but please think about it. I don't want you to resign. We can get past this."

"I can't, Kendell. Now, please just go."

Kendell didn't argue anymore. He moved to gather his things. "Listen, November, I'm sorry, and I hope that things work out with you, whatever you choose. Tell your husband that I will give every cent back to him soon."

November didn't respond. She didn't even look at him. He stood for a few more moments and then he left.

November went into the bedroom and climbed into the bed. She looked at the clock and called April. When her sister asked how Tracy's surprise trip to New York went, she lied and pretended that they were together and all was good. She was too embarrassed and had no clue what would happen next, so she didn't want April to worry about her.

After she was done talking to April and was satisfied the baby was okay, she called Tracy's cell phone and left him another message. She promised him that she would work it out with him and help him because she didn't want to be without him. In spite of it all, she loved him, and she wasn't ready to call it quits on her marriage.

She hugged the pillow and thought about Kendell. He was a good person. He was smart, ambitious, but most of all, he had been a friend to her. She didn't want to admit it, but she was going to miss him and miss working with him. She hated that she had to leave her job. And she was pissed at Tracy for ruining her job and her working relationship with Kendell. They were the perfect team, and she knew their business would have been a huge success.

Closing her eyes, she prayed and asked God to fix her marriage and bring her family back together. She wanted so much for her and Tracy to make it. She didn't want to be without him. She wanted them to work it out.

Chapter Twenty-six

The next morning, her wake-up call from the front desk got her up. She went to the bathroom and started the water then checked her cell phone. She was disappointed to see that Tracy hadn't called.

When she came out of the shower, she looked at the phone on the desk in the other room and saw the message light blinking. She rushed to listen to the messages, hoping one would be from Tracy, but the first one was from Kendell.

"Hey, November, this is Kendell. I know you don't have anything to say to me, but I wanted to tell you again how sorry I am. If there's ever a time you want to talk to me again, for any reason, please don't hesitate to call me." He went silent, but she could still hear him on the line. After a moment, he hung up.

The next message was from Tracy. "Hey, Novey. I, um . . . I, um . . . I would like for you to go home. I talked to April, and she told me that you said we may stay a few more days. I know why you lied, but I want you to go home. I will be in touch, so don't worry about me, okay? I love you, and I love TJ. Just please go home and leave me a voice mail when you make it. I love you, and please . . . please . . ." The voice mail time limit cut him short.

"No, no, no," November yelled. She slammed the phone down and started to sob. "Why didn't you call me back, Tracy? I need to talk to you," she cried. "I need to talk to you, dammit."

She sat on the floor and cried for a moment. Then she got up and dragged herself into the bedroom to dress. Seeming to move in slow motion, she packed up her things and went down to the lobby to check out.

The clerk pointed out the door. "The car is ready to take you to the airport, ma'am."

"Thank you," November said and walked out.

The limo driver got out to put her bags in the trunk. She looked at him and realized it was the same guy who had driven them around the day before and who had picked them up from the airport when they arrived.

"Excuse me?" she said.

"Yes, ma'am?" he answered.

"If your company picked up someone from here last night, is there any way I can find out where they dropped them?"

"Well, yes, but you'd have to talk to someone in our office." He stepped aside to shut her door.

"Can you take me by the agency?"

"I wish I could, but I'm on a schedule. After I drop you off at the airport, I have another pickup."

"Well, do you have a card with a number?"

"Sure," he said and reached into his jacket pocket. He pulled out a card, handed it to her, and shut the door.

She pulled out her cell phone and dialed the number.

"Mobil Trans, this is Jackie," the agent said.

"Hi, Jackie, how are you today?"

"I'm good, and yourself?"

"Just great. Listen, Jackie, I'm in a bit of a situation. I'm new to New York, and I got my wires crossed. I am November Stone. My husband is Tracy Stone. He arrived yesterday, and he has to stay over a couple more days for business. I am so disorganized, and I've misplaced the card of the hotel he is going to be staying in. Since he's in meetings today, I can't get him on his cell phone. Can you tell me what hotel your driver dropped him off at last night?" she asked politely with her fingers crossed.

"Tracy Stone, you said?"

"Yes, ma'am." She could hear the agent stroking the keyboard.

"Well, I would need a form of verification, Mrs. Stone. Would you happen to know the credit card number he used?"

"Was it a Visa or Discover?"

"No, it's an American Express."

November sighed. She had no idea what card that would be because Tracy had a few business cards. "Okay, ma'am, thanks. He has a dozen corporate cards, so I don't know."

"I'm sorry, ma'am. That is the only way I'd be able to give you that information."

"Thank you, Jackie, for your time," she said and hung up.

She had no clue where to even start looking for him, and it would take her forever to call every hotel in Manhattan, so she just accepted she had to wait for him to call her.

She rode to the airport, and it dawned on her that she didn't have a ride home when she got back to Chicago. She had ridden to the airport with Kendell. She'd have to get a cab, which would cost a small fortune. She pulled out her cell phone and called April, but got her machine. She reached her on her cell, but she said she couldn't come get her. She was shorthanded at the center and leaving for even ten minutes would be against regulations.

She scrolled through her list of contacts until she came across her sister-in-law Darlene's number. They weren't close, but they got along. Plus, Darlene was a housewife, so she was probably available.

"Hey, Darlene, this is Novey."

"Hey, Novey. How's everything?" Darlene asked pleasantly.

"Everything's okay, but I need a favor," November said.

"Okay."

"I'm coming into O'Hare about four, and I need someone to pick me up."

"Where is Tracy? I thought he was meeting you out there yesterday."

"Well, Darlene, it is a long story," November said.

Darlene didn't push the issue. "Okay, don't worry. I can come."

November gave her the flight information, and they hung up.

She sat back in the seat of the limo and popped a couple of Dramamine to keep from having the episode she had on her way to New York. She thought about Kendell and how sweet and helpful he was to her. He had kept her calm and made sure she was okay. She thought about how cool and calm he always was and how he was always positive. He was funny and made a joke about almost everything.

She'd miss working with him. He had the nerve to say he was in love with her. She shook her head. "Yeah, whatever," she said under her breath.

When she landed and Darlene had driven her home, she was exhausted mentally and physically. She wondered when her husband would be coming home.

"Thanks, Darlene, you are a lifesaver," she said, putting her bags down.

"No problem, girl. I'd do almost anything to have some time away from the boys." She laughed.

"I can only imagine having three boys and Trent under one roof."

"Yes, chile. My biggest dilemma is the bathroom. Them slobs can't aim for shit," she said, and they laughed.

"You want a drink?" November offered her.

"Yes, ma'am." Darlene walked over to the center island in November's huge kitchen. The room was massive, and as always, clean as a whistle. "Girl, I've always loved your kitchen," she said. "The only thing I hate about my house is the kitchen. We have over thirty-six hundred square feet, and I think the kitchen is only five square feet." She laughed.

November laughed a little, but she was down, and she wasn't in the mood to joke around. She poured them both wine, took a couple swallows of hers, then topped off the glass and took another sip.

"Novey, what is it?" Darlene asked. She looked and sounded concerned.

"Huh?" November looked at her sister-in-law through teary eyes.

"Come on, Novey, you can talk to me. Come on and sit down and tell me what's wrong." She took November by the hand, and they went into the family room and sat down.

"Whew, Lord, Darlene," November said, looking up at the ceiling. She didn't want to cry, but she couldn't hold back. "I don't know. I mean, I don't understand why Tracy is so, so, so insanely jealous. He doesn't know how to trust. I mean, no matter what I do or say, he is constantly thinking that I'm cheating or gonna cheat. He's been lying to me for months, having me think that things were fine and that he was better, but he tried to set me up."

"Set you up? What do you mean, set you up?" Darlene asked.

November painfully gave her the details of
what had happened. When she was done, she
was more upset than she was when she started.

"Aww, November, we didn't know Tracy was
this bad."

"What do you mean 'this bad'?"

"Tracy never told you, did he?"

"Told me what, Darlene?" November wiped
her tears.

"About how his daddy died?"

"Yes, he told me his dad had a heart attack
when he was younger, and his mom died shortly
after."

"No, baby, that's not what happened. Trenton
and Tracy's dad was killed by one of their
mother's lovers. And Tracy's momma isn't dead,
November. They just haven't spoken to her in
over fifteen years. She lives in Oak Brook."

"No, no, that's not what Tracy told me,"
November said, shaking her head.

Darlene got up and poured herself another
glass of wine and brought the bottle over to the
table and poured more in November's glass.

"Okay. Well, let me tell you what really happened. When they were younger, their daddy,
Melvin, started that towing company from
nothing. He worked long and hard hours, and he
was always gone. When the business grew and

money started to flow, he then opened a used car lot, and that led him to work even longer hours. He had Trent and Tracy with him, working all the time either towing cars or at the car lot, and when the lot grew and turned into a small dealership, it was all about work and not about his marriage, leaving Treva all alone. Eventually, she started to mess around.

"Melvin and Treva argued a lot because he became too wrapped up in work to cater to his wife, and things got bad. She'd let her lovers pick her up at the house. This continued as the boys got older. Treva was more and more unhappy, and she became out of control with her affairs to the point where she no longer tried to hide them. One day, Tracy walked in on his momma having sex in the garage with this man named Joseph Tucker, and he told his daddy. Melvin decided to follow Treva one night, and he had the boys in the car with him.

"He had his gun and swore that he was gon' kill that man if he caught him with his wife. So he followed her to Joseph's house, and when she parked and went inside, their daddy waited for a while then he went and knocked on the man's door. When Joseph opened the door, their daddy pushed his way in and found Treva in the man's bed, naked. Melvin pulled out that gun on that man and they got to tussling in Joseph's living room and it somehow fell in their struggle. Joseph picked it up and shot Melvin three times.

"Trent and Tracy heard all three shots, and then they heard their momma screaming. They got out of the car and ran into Joseph's house and saw their daddy lying on the floor in a pool of blood and their momma at his side with a sheet around her naked body. That crazy Joseph got on his clothes and ran before the police got there, and their daddy was dead before he made it to the hospital. Since Joseph Tucker fled the scene and their daddy was shot three times, as opposed to just once, he was charged with manslaughter. He tried but didn't get off on self-defense, even though the gun belonged to Melvin.

"By the time Trenton turned sixteen and Tracy was thirteen, they left to live with their grandma because they didn't wanna live with their momma anymore. They found out that their daddy had changed everything and didn't leave their momma a cent. Not even the house. When they were old enough to handle their affairs, they sold the house and split the profit. Trent took over the car dealership, and Tracy took over the towing business.

"Melvin knew a lot of people in Chicago, and after it was all said and done, Trent and Tracy were set for life, because he had contacts and friends all over who were there to care for them after he died. So, since I can remember, neither one of them has seen their mother or had anything to do with her, because of their daddy dying behind her affairs. The only reason I can think of why Tracy is like that is because of his momma. Yes, he's had unfaithful girlfriends, but I think its Treva's infidelity that got him like that."

November couldn't believe Tracy had lied to her about his parents. She remembered asking him about his mother on several occasions and him never wanting to talk about her. He always had wonderful memories and great things to say about his daddy, but he never wanted to talk about his momma.

"So why is Trent okay and Tracy is, I don't know, just messed up?"

"I don't know, Novey. Maybe because Trent was older when it happened. I'm not sure why Tracy is letting this haunt him like that."

"Why didn't he tell me the truth, Darlene? I wanna help him."

"Novey, trust me, my husband used to do the same thing to me. He used to keep tabs on me and would constantly want to know where I was, but that shit got old. It took me leaving his ass one time for him to straighten up. Now, we are fine. I try to get him to call his momma, and he gets angry and walks off and treats me like I cussed him out. But I just learned to pray for him and be there for him and not push, you know?"

"Tracy didn't give me a chance. He didn't tell me what happened."

"Trent didn't tell me either, honey. His grandma told me way back before she passed, when I used to have issues with Trent wanting to know my every move. One day, I was at her house helping her cook and Trent must have called me fifteen times to check on me. If I hadn't said, 'Grammy, I don't know why my husband is so insecure,' I may have never known it either."

"Well, I'm glad you told me, Darlene. Now I can try to reach him. I love him so much, and I don't want him torturing himself."

"I know you love him, Novey, and he loves you so much. He and Trent are close and they talk. He expresses his love for you every time he talks about you and that little boy."

"How do I help him, Darlene? What if I can't?"

"November, for one, pray. Two, be patient because your husband is a good man and I know you guys are gonna be all right. I know this doctor Trent and I saw a few years back, and it helped. I will call you later and give you a number, but you have to be willing to try."

"I am, Darlene. I just need to get through to Tracy." Tears rolled down her cheeks.

"You will, babe. Trust me, you will," Darlene said. "Don't worry; just pray. It will be okay. When he comes home, just take it one day at a time. And you've got to forgive him for this foolish game he played with you, November. If you can't, you might as well throw in the towel right now."

Chapter Twenty-seven

Three days later, November still hadn't heard from Tracy. She felt like it was over for them. If he didn't miss her or think it was necessary to call her, she didn't feel she should continue to call him, so she stopped calling and texting him. She had gotten a few private calls on her cell and figured it was Kendell, but he never said a word when she answered.

She decided to get dressed and comb her hair. She hadn't picked her son up because she had hoped to hear from Tracy and that he'd come home so they could talk. But since that hadn't happened, she wanted to go get her baby. She hadn't seen him since she had gotten home because she was in no shape to take care of him. She drove to April's in a daze, wondering what was next for her and Tracy.

"Hey, baby boy," she said, picking him up and holding him close. "Did you miss me? Huh? Did you miss me, sweetie?"

TJ laughed. She was so happy to see her baby. And she could tell he missed her. She held him tight and gave him a million kisses. He was so happy and excited to see her that he was giggling and patting her face.

"How was he?" she asked April.

"Perfect. He was just perfect," her sister said. She picked up her daughter. "How are you holding up?"

"I'm good, babe. Just hanging in there and praying."

"That's good. I'm glad you finally told me what was going on. You didn't have to lie to me, Shareese. I'm your sister, and I am here for you no matter what it is, so don't ever be afraid or embarrassed to tell me anything. I am married too, and I know marriage isn't a walk in the park."

"I know, sis. I just don't know what to do. I mean, I love him so much, and I hoped he'd come home by now. I just don't know if we are gonna make it."

"You will. It's just seems bad right now, but I promise you it is going to be okay. I can see a happy ending."

"Come on, April, don't soup me up with your predictions and psychic visions. This is my marriage, and I'm terrified that it is over."

"November Shareese, don't say that. I'm not feeding you no mumbo jumbo. I'm for real. And I am so sure that this is gonna work out. Trust me. And when this is all over, you gon' stop calling me crazy and recognize that I do see things. When I look at you, there is a bright background with rays of light, meaning that this will pass. I've seen gloom on folks, honey, and I knew that tragedy was coming. But this is just your test. You and Tracy will have a happy ending, I promise."

November smiled. "Thanks, sis. You always know what to say and do. And I know you're not crazy. I just don't have the gift of seeing what's to come, and right now, I'm frightened that my marriage is over. I don't think I'll be able to help him."

"Listen to me. This is far from over. You and your husband are just going through a rough patch. You are doing what you are supposed to do, and that's praying. So start trusting and believing that God is working it out for you. Don't make me call your daddy on you, 'cause you know Daddy will hit you with the Word," she said, teasing.

November laughed. As odd as her family was, they believed that God was in control. "No, please don't call Daddy." April laughed with her.

"Tracy loves you. I knew he was gon' marry you from the day I met him. And I see you and him having a little sister for TJ, too. I feel it, so don't worry. It is going to work out."

"Oh, yeah? And what about the farm and all that other mess you told my husband before we got married?"

"Chile, I was just messing with him wit' that. I got jokes, too," she said, and they laughed.

"Girl, let me get my baby's coat so we can get back to the house." While April went to get his things, November put on his coat, went to her SUV, and loaded him into his car seat.

She drove home listening to Mary J. Blige's "Be Without You" on repeat. She stopped at a red light and looked over her shoulder at her baby sleeping so peacefully. When she got home, her house was cold and empty. She wished her husband were home.

She took TJ up to his nursery and put his nightclothes on and put him in his crib. In her bedroom, she picked up the phone and checked the caller ID. No calls from Tracy. She went downstairs and poured a glass of wine, turned on the stereo, and picked the smooth R&B station on her satellite radio. "The Way" by Jill Scott was playing. She sat on the sofa with her glass in one hand and the bottle in the other.

"Tracy, please call me," she said out loud.

When nothing happened, she got up and looked out the window. She stood there frozen, looking for Tracy to pull up. But he didn't. Her cell phone rang, and she dashed to get it from her purse. The ID showed it was another private call. She answered it, hoping it was her husband.

"Hello," she said. No one said anything. "Hello," she said again. Still silence. As soon as she was about to hang up, he spoke up.

"November, please don't hang up," Kendell said.

"What do you want?" she asked sharply. She wondered why he was calling her. She had made it clear she didn't want to talk to him ever again.

"I need to talk to you, Novey."

"About what, Kendell?"

"Listen, November, I know you hate me, and I know I'm not one of your favorite people right now, but I need to know if you forgive me. Please. I am going crazy not being able to talk to you. I know that is something I'll have to get over, but please, I want you to know I am sorry. I am. And I wish I could do it all over again differently."

"Well, Kendell, understand this: I don't care what you are going through. Do you think I'm not going through it too? Do you think all is well in my life now? I can't blame you for everything, but you played a part in deceiving me. You went along with a foolish scheme that you allowed to go on. You and my husband treated me like I was a whore, and I haven't gotten past that just yet, okay?"

"I know, November, and—"

"And what, Kendell? You love me? Really? If you cared about me, you would have told me what was going on. I'm just so angry with you and Tracy for what y'all thought was a great idea to do to me. My marriage is in the balance right now," she cried. "I still love a man who paid someone to seduce me. I want to not love him, but I love my husband in spite of what he has done to me. And I do, Kendell, I . . . I do forgive you. But you shouldn't call me anymore. We have nothing to talk about or discuss. We cannot be friends, and I'm sorry that my husband dragged you into our dysfunctional marriage. I wish you well, but please don't call me again."

"November, I know we can't be friends, and what I feel for you may not ever change, but I want what I've always wanted for you, and that is for you to be happy. If you don't want me to ever contact you again, I won't."

"That's best, Kendell."

"Okay then. I wish you well, November. Take care of yourself, and I hope you and Tracy work things out."

"Thanks, Kendell. You have a nice life." She hung up and cried after their conversation because at least Kendell was concerned about her. Not that she could say the same for Tracy.

She dropped her phone on the floor and picked up the wine bottle that was on the coffee table. It barely had enough in it to halfway fill her glass, so she went over to the wine cooler and grabbed another bottle of chardonnay and opened it.

After two more glasses, she was feeling good, so she picked up her cell phone and called Tracy. After it rang five times, his voice mail came on again. She hit end and then threw the phone on the sofa. She wanted to scream at the top of her lungs, but her son was upstairs sleeping. *Calm down, Shareese,* she told herself, fighting tears. *It's gon' be okay. It's gon' be just fine. This will be over soon.*

"No matter what, you got you," she told herself as she climbed the stairs.

She peeped in on her baby and smiled at the sight of his little body sleeping in his crib. She watched his fat, round little belly go up and down as he slept, then she eased her head out and pulled his door closed a little. She went back downstairs to turn off the stereo and put her glass in the sink. She rinsed it and wondered what she was going to do with herself if she and Tracy didn't get back together.

As much as she loved her husband, she was starting to feel bitter toward him because of what he was doing to her. At that moment, she told herself that it may not work, and if she wasn't able to help him, she would have to just move on with her life. She wanted to be in a normal relationship with someone who loved her and she could love back. That was simple enough for her. She felt that if the love were strong in his heart for her, he'd come home.

She was about to turn out the lights when she heard her baby crying. She sprinted up the steps and picked him up. "It's okay, baby, Mommy's here," she said, rocking him.

"Dah, dah, dah, dah," he said, looking around and reaching in the direction of the door. "Dah, dah, dah, dah." He squirmed in November's arms.

"Shhh, baby, Daddy's not here. What's wrong, TJ?" she asked when he seemed to throw a tantrum. "What is it?"

He twisted and pulled away like he wanted her to put him down. "Dah, dah, dah, dah," he said again.

"Look now, TJ, you better stop it," she said firmly, and he calmed down. She kissed him on the cheek, and he rested his head on her shoulder. She kissed his head and swayed with him in her arms. "That's my little man. You tried to cut up on Mommy. That's what you were trying to do, huh? I know you miss your daddy, baby. Mommy misses him too."

She walked him back down the steps with her to set the alarm.

She went back up and put him in a fresh diaper and decided to put him in bed with her. He fell asleep, and she drifted off to sleep shortly after he did.

Chapter Twenty-eight

The next morning, November and TJ were up early. She was in the kitchen fixing him eggs and grits, and he was in the family room on the floor. When she came around the counter to get him, she found him standing up all by himself. She froze and watched as he took one step and then another and then another before he fell on his bottom.

"TJ, baby, you walked," she said picking him up and dancing around. "You walked, little man." He laughed as she lifted him up in the air. "Oh, my goodness. I gotta call your daddy."

Her smile faded when she remembered he was gone. She kissed her baby, put him back down, and went back into the kitchen to get his breakfast.

She put TJ in his high chair and tried not to think of Tracy. After she was done feeding him and cleaning up his mess, she called April to tell her the good news. Mother and son spent the day together, and by the afternoon, her son was walking around like a professional. Over the next couple of days, all she did was play with her baby and struggle not to think about her absent husband.

It had been nine days since she heard from him. How could he just not call or say anything to her? How could he not call and check on his son? He had missed their child taking his first step, something major, and he missed out on it because of his foolish and selfish ways. She refocused and shifted her thoughts to another place, because every time she thought about him, she got mad.

She turned out the lights, took her son upstairs, and gave him a bath and rocked him to sleep. Then she took a long, hot shower and dried off. She put lotion on and stood in front of the mirror looking at her reflection. She rubbed her hand across her tummy over all the stretch marks and wondered how she would get another man at her age with a son. She wasn't the young, sexy twenty-five-year-old woman she had been. Imagining what dating would be like at her age and starting all over again made her cringe. She looked at her face closely and smiled. She was a pretty woman. She wondered why it took Tracy to come into her life for her to realize that she was beautiful.

She put on her PJs and climbed into her empty bed. She felt so lonely, and she wished Tracy were there to hold her close through the night. *Hell, some dick would be nice, too.* She grabbed her novel from the nightstand drawer. She opened it and began to read before she drifted off to sleep.

By the third week of no husband, she was not only getting used to being without Tracy, but she had accepted that he wasn't coming back. She had her moments, but she was able to refocus herself. She wasn't stressing about him anymore. The money was still there, and their bills were paid. Tracy hadn't taken her off any of their accounts or frozen their money, so she was okay.

She went on the Internet to look around and see what jobs were out there because she knew she would have to get a job if Tracy decided he wanted out. She still wanted her own business, though. She might also have to look for a more affordable house, but she wasn't ready to go to that extreme just yet. It wasn't like he had given her divorce papers.

She looked at her baby and smiled and wondered why she was even thinking about a job when she had him. He was still small, and it was nice to be at home with him.

Kendell used to always tell her that if she wanted to start her own business, he'd show her the ropes. Now that they weren't even speaking, that wasn't something she could count on anymore. But she was still determined. She made up her mind. She was going to do it. She was going to use this time to gather her resources and do it.

She went online again, this time looking at office spaces for lease. Then she decided to call Jonathan because he would be of help in the real estate department. She got his voice mail and had to leave him a message to call her back. She was going back to the computer when her doorbell rang. That was odd because nobody ever came to her house. And if someone was coming over, they'd call.

She looked through the peephole and saw the FedEx guy, so she opened the door and signed for the package. She opened it and found a check from Kendell's company to Tracy. A note was clipped to it.

Trey, here is your money. How I let you talk me into doing what I did is beyond me. That's not who I am, and I'm so ashamed of what went down. Understand this: November is a good woman, and she didn't deserve any of this. If you don't stop and realize that for yourself, you are gonna

lose her and then you will be sorrier than
what you already are.

   I know I owe you more for November's
investment, and you will get it soon, I
swear on my life. After that, you will never
hear from me again. Take care of her, man,
and I know it is a stretch, but try to make
her happy, because she deserves to be
happy.
   Kendell Gordon

She looked at the check, and her eyes popped.
She could see why he had taken Tracy up on
his offer. It was more than enough money to
start her own business. She went back to the
computer and continued to look at office spaces,
then decided to look for a new place to live. She
decided to look for something with the option
to have an office space downstairs and maybe a
condo or loft upstairs. That would help her and
be more convenient for her to start. That way,
she would just be paying one mortgage.

After she surfed for a while, she decided she'd
wait for Jonathan to call her and she'd tell
him what she was looking for. She got dressed
and dressed her son, and they went to the
bank and deposited the check that Kendell had
sent into an account that Tracy didn't monitor or question. He had opened the account for

November that had a direct deposit of $1,000 a month for November to shop and get her hair, nails, or whatever she chose done, without her having to go to him for petty cash. His name was on the account, but after the bank card came, he handed it to her and told her to set up her own online login, and he had never once asked her about the account. Chances were he'd never check the account.

They went by the mall and shopped a little and then went to the grocery store to get a few items. She was on her way home when her cell phone rang. It was Darlene.

"Hey, Darlene," November said, turning down the radio.

"Hey, how are you and the baby?"

"We are good. How are you?"

"Girl, drained and tired."

"I know the feeling."

"Yes, ma'am. I called you to tell you the news."

November thought it might be about Tracy. "What news?"

"Well, I'm pregnant. Again."

"Wow. Get outta here."

"I know, right? I just hope this one is a girl because, after this, I'm getting fixed."

"Well, I hope you get your girl outta this one."

"Even if I don't, I'm still getting fixed."

"I know that's right."

"Yes, and the other thing I called to tell you is I overheard Trent talking to Tracy this morning," she said low. "Now, I don't know where he is actually staying, but I've been working on it for you. I do know he is in Chicago, and, Novey, he's been seeing someone."

"My husband is cheating on me?" November yelled.

"No, no, no. I'm talking about a doctor. I overheard Trent asking him how his sessions were going."

"Oh, Darlene, thank God."

"I just thought you should know. I have been on Trent, but he won't tell me nothing."

"Thank you for calling. I miss him so much, and I am just glad to know that he is all right and he is getting help. You don't know how relieved I am to hear that."

"I know, baby, but don't worry. Be patient. It will all work out."

November's eyes welled. "Thanks, Darlene."

"Listen, Trent is coming up the stairs. As soon as I know something, I'll call you."

"Okay, thanks again." November ended the call and cried all the way home. *Why won't he just call to say something?* she wondered.

When she got in and got settled, she decided she couldn't wait for Darlene. She called Trent herself.

"Hey, Novey, what's going on?" he asked.

"Don't 'what's up' me, Trenton Lorenz Stone. Where is he?" she demanded.

"Where is who?"

"Don't play games with me, Trent. I know you know where Tracy is, and I need to talk to him."

"I don't know where he's staying, November, I promise. He won't tell me either."

"Please don't do this to me. I need to talk to him. He hasn't called in three weeks, and I'm going crazy without my husband."

"November, for real, I don't know where he is. He will not tell me. I just talk to him on the phone. That is it."

"Can you find out for me please, Trent? This is my marriage we are talking about. This is my husband. I'm not some deranged girlfriend. I miss my husband. I need my husband. My son needs his daddy to come home. Can you please tell him that for me, Trent? Can you tell him I love him no matter what and I'm dying without him?"

"November, I know, and I'm sorry you are going through what you are going through, but I can't promise you anything. I've told him time and time again to go home, and I've told him time and time again to call you."

"Trent, do you love your wife?"

"Of course I do," he said.

"Tell me something: if Darlene left you and didn't talk to you for weeks because you were having problems, how would you feel?"

"It would mess me up," he admitted.

"That's the thing, Trent. I'm messed up, and I need Tracy in my life, no matter what. So please call him and tell him that for me. Tell him I love him," she said, crying into the phone.

"November, I will call him, and I will tell him everything you said. I promise I will."

"Thank you, Trent," she said, sniffling.

She hung up and fell on her knees and cried. She begged God to help them and to put it in Tracy's heart to come home.

Chapter Twenty-nine

Tracy's cell phone rang, and he saw it was Trent. He picked up on the second ring. He always talked to Trent, because he wanted to make sure that November and the baby were okay. If anything went wrong, Trent would know about it.

"Trent, what's going on?" he said.

"You need to call her," Trent said.

"Why? Is everything okay? Is my son okay?" he asked, panicking.

"No, everything is not okay, Tracy. Your wife is messed up right now. You need to go home and be there for her. She loves you, man, and she is going through a lot, Trey. Go home to your family. They need you."

"I can't, man, not right now."

"You can, Trey, damn. She is in terrible shape. You act like it's all about you and your problems, but your problems are her problems. You need to stop this bullshit and go home."

"I can't face her, man. I'm not the man she deserves right now."

"Trey, nobody's perfect. She loves you, man, and she wants you to come home. She forgives you, Tracy, and she misses you. Your son needs you. Now get your head out'cha ass and go home to your family. We all make mistakes. Don't you understand that November is not our mother? She is not Brianna. She is the woman you married, who you took vows to be there for through it all. But you are off somewhere in your own madness, feeling sorry for yourself. You are not Pop. Pop put his business first and his wife last. Mom, as wrong as she was, needed him and he wasn't there for her.

"Don't do that to your wife, man. Don't leave her out there alone like Pop did to our mother. I am not defending her, but our father didn't do what he was supposed to do, Tracy, and she was lonely. The longer you stay away, the lonelier your wife will become. And if she moves on, Tracy, that will be your loss.

"She forgives you. It takes a strong woman to stay after what you did, and if she is willing to work shit out with you after the shit you pulled, you ought to be praising God. Now go your ass home to your wife and son."

"I can't, Trent," Tracy said, crying.

"Tracy, do you love November?"

"Yes, I love my wife. What kinda question is that?"

"If you love her, you will go home and do what families do: work it out. You are a married man. You are not a single person, and you can't do November like you did all those other chicks you couldn't bring yourself to trust. You can't go off and be by yourself and push them away so you can put them in this 'women ain't no good' category. She is your wife and the best thing that ever happened to you. Now, if you don't wise up and go home and work it out with her, you may not have that opportunity later on."

"Trent, I just don't know if I'm ready, man. How can I face her?"

"Look, li'l brother, I know it's gonna be hard, but at least call her. Let her tell you herself what the first step is. I promised my sister-in-law that I'd tell you what she told me to tell you and that is, 'I love you and come home.'"

"She said that?"

"Yes, and that she needs her husband. Now, when I hang up, *call your wife*."

"Trent, what do I say? I don't know how to start."

"You can start by telling her you love her and that everything is going to be okay. Once you hear Novey's voice, trust me when I tell you it will come to you. I know you guys are gon' make it, Trey. Just call her."

"I hear ya," Tracy said.

"Okay, li'l brother. I love you, and I wish you and November the best. And by the way, Darlene's pregnant."

"Damn, dude, let me catch up." Tracy chuckled.

"Go your ass home and maybe you will."

"I hear ya, bro. Thank you, Trent, and I love you. Tell Darlene congratulations."

"Okay, I'm out," Trent said and hung up.

Tracy took a deep breath and dialed his house. His hands shook. He got more nervous when the phone started to ring. He hoped she'd talk to him and not cuss him out too bad.

"Tracy, baby, where are you?" were her first words. No hello.

"I'm okay, Novey. How is TJ?" he asked.

"He's fine, baby. He just misses his daddy. Tracy, please, when are you coming home?"

"Novey, I want to come home—"

"Then come home, then. Come home right now," she said, crying. "I can't do this anymore, Tracy. We need you to come home."

"I know, baby, and I miss you guys so much." Tracy cried with her. He couldn't stand to hear her cry like that.

"I miss you too, Tracy, and I want you so much. I need you so much."

"Novey, I know I've been a horrible husband. I've done things that I'm not proud of, and, baby, I wanna come home more than you know. But before I do, you must understand that we have a long road ahead of us."

"I do understand that, Tracy, and we cannot work things out apart. How can you be away from us and not miss us?"

"Baby, I do miss you and TJ. It kills me each day to be without you two."

"Tracy, I never asked you to leave," she said defensively.

"I know you didn't, but I had to get my head right. You may not understand why, but I had to do some thinking and talk to somebody to get my mind right. I still have a long way to go."

"Okay then, Tracy. I'm not gon' beg you to come home, but I have a question for you. Do you want to work this marriage out or do you want to continue to go at this alone? We are married. You are not married to yourself, so you shouldn't have to go through this by yourself. If that is your choice and you are going to treat this like it's just your problem, you don't need me, and I'm not going to sit here and keep crying and stressing myself out over our marriage. I just can't do it. Now, do you want this marriage? Because if you don't, tell me so I can move on with my life."

"Baby, I do need you. I need you so much, and I don't want to continue to be by myself. I want you and I want my son."

"Then why am I here alone without my husband? Why is the man I love not including me in his life? Tracy, I love you. If I didn't, I wouldn't give a damn if you ever came home. But I'm here willing to fight for us and work this out. I'm right here."

"You love me that much, November?"

"Yes, Tracy," she said, sobbing. "I love you just that much."

"Baby, I'm so sorry for everything," he said.

"Tracy, just come home."

"I'll be there soon."

"I can't wait to see you."

"I love you, November."

November rushed upstairs to shower and fix herself up. She was so excited she couldn't contain herself. Although it was late, she put on makeup and fixed her hair. She put on a pretty lingerie set and sprayed his favorite Bath & Body Works fragrance on her skin. She lit candles and opened a bottle of wine and sat on the couch, nervously waiting for her husband. Her son was asleep, so he would have to see his daddy in the morning, which was fine with her because she wanted him all to herself.

Chapter Thirty

Tracy pulled into the garage and parked his Infiniti between his Benz and November's SUV. They had a four-car garage, but it still seemed kind of tight at times. He got out and decided not to get any of his things. He was anxious to see his family.

He went inside and stepped into the kitchen. The candles lit the room, and the fragrance reminded him how much he missed being home. When he saw Novey looking like a queen, he immediately remembered why he fell in love with her. She was wearing a plum two-piece number that he had always loved her in.

"You are so beautiful, November," he said.

She smiled. "So are you."

She moved to the cabinet and took out a glass for him then went to the fridge and grabbed the bottle she had started. She was about to pour it for him, but he came closer to her.

"Let me get that," he said. He opened the bottle and poured some in his glass and topped hers off and handed it to her. He felt awkward as they drank.

"Come on," he said and took her hand. He led her into the family room, and they sat down. "Look, Novey, I'm sorry for all the bullshit I put you through. I was an insecure fool, and I am so ashamed of myself. The thought of another man touching you—"

"Shhh, don't say that. Don't let that thought enter your mind. I know you have experienced and witnessed a few women disappointing you, and I know it was hard for you to picture a woman being opposite of those types of women, but life is full of good and bad people. All women are not the same, and all men are not the same either. Love makes you do crazy things. Love gives you strength to forgive. Love also gives you the power to trust. Love, Tracy, gives you the motivation to move on. I know our love has what it takes to make it through this. It's gonna take some work, but I'm willing."

"I'm willing too, but I'm so afraid, November, that nothing will help me. I feel like even going to a shrink won't help me because when we are not in the same room, my mind goes back to my mother and my exes. I swear I don't mean to take it out on you."

"Listen, Tracy, I don't have the cure or any magic potion that I can give you to make it better. All I can tell you is that I'm gonna be right here and we will find a solution. In time, you'll get better, but what you have to start doing for me is fighting. Every time those images enter your mind, you say, 'November is not my mother or Brianna,' and you continue to fight that demon until you are free."

"I will, Novey, because I know in my heart who you are. I know that you are not my mother. One thing I've learned since I've been going to therapy is that I need to forgive her and understand that she is human too and she made some bad decisions. Unfortunately, my daddy had to lose his life because of a decision she made, but it's over. Treva doing what she did, or Brianna doing what she did, doesn't make you a liar. It's simple on one hand, Novey, and I know I can beat this."

"So do it, baby. You are gonna be just fine. *We* are gonna be fine." November smiled.

"I love you, November."

"I love you too, baby," she said, and they kissed.

They put down their glasses and kissed each other passionately. They soon went from passion to hunger and November trembled under Tracy's touch.

"Baby, I've missed you so much," he whispered as he undid the little button holding her top closed.

"I've missed you too," she said, reaching for his belt. They kissed each other, and within seconds, they were both undressed. They were starving for each other. Tracy sucked on her erect nipples as he entered her. It had been awhile since they had made love, so it was short but sweet.

She smiled at him, and he buried his face in her breasts like he was embarrassed. She kissed the top of his head, and they lay there for a few moments with no words. They just inhaled each other and listened to the soft music.

It felt good just to be home. They finally got up and went upstairs. Before they went into their room, Tracy went in to see his son. He picked him up, even though he was sleeping, and kissed him a couple of times before he put him back down.

When he got into their bedroom, November was already under the covers waiting for him. He climbed into bed and vowed that he'd never leave his family again. He held November tight, and before long, he was inside of her again. They made love through the night, and the next morning, he got up with the baby and let his wife sleep in.

Tracy could tell that his son had missed him. He tried to put him down so he could make breakfast, but TJ didn't want him to put him down. He fought with him as he tried to put him in his playpen, so he picked him up again and sat on the sofa. He turned on the TV and sat TJ on the side of him. He waited 'til the baby was occupied with the TV and then eased into the kitchen.

A few minutes later, TJ walked into the kitchen. When Tracy realized his son was walking, he yelled for November to get up. She ran downstairs in her robe, trying to figure out what was wrong.

"Baby, TJ walked into the kitchen, I swear," Tracy said and put him down so November could see.

"I know, baby. He started walking a couple of weeks ago," November said, yawning. She went for the coffee.

"What? I missed his first step?" Tracy asked.

"Yep, you missed it," she said, putting cream into her cup. She took a seat on a stool at the island.

"Well, I'll be damned," Tracy said putting both palms down on the island, shaking his head. "I missed my son taking his first steps."

"Baby, it's okay. It was just a few days ago."

"No, it's not okay, Novey."

"Listen, baby, don't start beating yourself up, okay? You are home now, and you will have the rest of his life to catch all of his firsts."

"That's not the point." He poured pancake batter onto the griddle.

"Baby, come on. We are going to take one day at a time," she said, hopping off the stool. She went over and hugged him, and he gave her a smile.

"You're right."

"Yep. Now, hurry up, I'm starving," she said and popped him on his bottom.

They ate and laughed like everything had been fine all along. They didn't talk about Kendell or their problems; they just enjoyed themselves. They stayed at the house and just hung around as a family watching movies, and she and Tracy played a few games of dominos. When they put TJ down for his nap, they played around in their room for a couple of hours, making up for lost time.

"You are an extraordinary woman, November," he said, holding her hand.

"You are an exceptional man, Tracy. Things are gonna be fine. Just give us some time."

"I know," he said and smiled.

"I'm so glad you're home, baby." She smiled.

"So am I. I am so sorry for everything."

She sat up. "I know, baby, and things will be better for us. Marriages are not a walk in the park."

"You got that right."

She smiled. "Well, I'm going to head down and make some dinner."

"Okay. Let me check on TJ and then I'll be down to help."

"No, baby, I got it."

"Well, I can at least keep you company."

"Yes, I'd like that." She smiled and gave him one more quick kiss before heading downstairs.

After dinner, November cleaned the kitchen while Tracy took care of the baby. It felt like things were back to normal, and she felt positive that things were going to be okay. She thought about April and what she said, and she smiled. *Maybe she does have a gift,* she thought as she started the dishwasher. Afterward, she went up to check on her men. Tracy was putting the baby down, so she went to take a shower.

"Hey, sexy," Tracy said, stepping into the shower with November.

"Hey, baby. You come to get dirty or clean?"

"I came to get dirty," he said, and she laughed.

"Oh, my," she said, allowing him to embrace her from behind.

They played around and washed each other's bodies. Tracy rubbed November's stomach with her bath sponge, looking at her stretch marks.

"Let's have another baby," he said.

"What?" November said, raising an eyebrow.

"Let's have another baby. Let's give TJ a little brother."

"Baby, come on. TJ is barely a year old."

"He'll be one in a couple of weeks, Novey. He and his brother can grow up close like Trent and I did."

"Whoa, hold on, Tracy. Slow down, baby. Don't get ahead of ourselves. I want more kids, but we have some work to do on our marriage. And I still want to start my own business."

"We can still do all those things, baby, and I'm here to have your back with whatever. So why not?"

"Because, Tracy, we have to think about some things. To just get pregnant now may not be the right thing to do."

"Why not? You love me, don't you?"

"Of course I do, baby, but that's not the question. It's just that we just got back together and we have some things we need to iron out first. We have plenty of time to have more kids."

"Yeah, you're right. We are still young. We can wait a little while," he agreed.

"Yes, we can. When the time is right, we will know it."

"Well, we can at least practice, right?"

"Oh, yes, that we can do."

Chapter Thirty-one

"Hey, come on in," November said, letting April and her family in and taking their coats. She and Tracy were having their son's first birthday party. Tracy wore a party hat, looking foolish, like a big kid. He walked into the foyer at the very moment Tony, April's husband, leaned in to kiss November on her cheek. Jealousy tried to rise up in him, but he was learning to relax, and he pushed the thoughts away.

"Hey, Tony. Man, what's going on wit'cha?" he asked and shook his brother-in-law's hand.

"Aww, man, same ol' same. Working, trying to take care of a houseful of spending women," he said, joking.

"I hear that."

"Baby, I'm gonna put these coats in the guest room," November said.

"Oh, let me help you with those," Tony said. Tracy almost knocked him down, pushing past him to get to November first.

"Naw, man, you are a guest. We got it," he said, taking some of the coats from November. He followed her down the hall into the guest bedroom.

"Tracy, what was that?" she asked when they were alone.

"What was what?"

"You almost knocked the man down."

"No, I didn't," he said defensively.

"Baby, relax. It's just Tony, my sister's husband. Don't let your mind wander off into something that ain't an issue." Their therapist had told them to confront any issues head-on. November was to bring it to Tracy's attention when she felt he was seeing what he wanted to see and not what it really was.

"Okay, baby, you're right. I was trippin', but I'm cool."

"Good," she said and kissed him. "And you need to take off that goofy-looking hat." She laughed.

"Man, don't hate. I look good in this hat." He followed her back into the kitchen.

During the party, Tracy tried not to watch November's every move, but it was hard. He was used to observing men who talked to his wife to make sure there was nothing fishy going on. It was hard for him to do otherwise, but he managed.

Before, he'd made sure he stood within earshot of any conversation she carried on with someone of the opposite sex. Now, he was learning to control that urge. Every man at his son's party was from the dealership or the towing companies, and they were with their wives and kids, but he still had to fight to keep his mind positive.

The evening progressed, and the children got restless and cranky. Soon it was time for people to start leaving. After all the children were gone, a couple of childless adults were still there. Tracy went up to get TJ ready for bed and November went to the kitchen to get more drinks for their remaining guests.

"Hey, November, what do you need me to grab?" Jonathan said.

"Oh, I got it, Jonathan. I think I can manage."

"Are you sure?"

"Yes. Unless you wanna grab those glasses for me."

"Sure," he said, putting them on a tray. "Before I forget, I tried calling you back a couple weeks ago. You had left a message on my voice mail about looking at some office spaces?"

Tracy walked in. "Hey, what's up?" he asked with a brow raised. November knew that look. She was sure Jonathan knew it too.

"Nothing, baby. Jonathan just came to give me a hand with the drinks," she said, not addressing Jonathan's question about the call.

"Yeah, I came to give her a hand," he said. He grabbed the tray and went back into the living room. She thanked God he hadn't said anything, but she knew that didn't settle right with Tracy.

They went back to their guests, but November could tell Tracy was upset. She hated that he had come in on her alone in the kitchen with Jonathan of all people.

As soon as they locked the door after their last guest, she turned to him to give him a hug, but he backed up.

"What's wrong?" she asked. *Here we go.*

"You tell me," he said sharply.

"I can't read your mind, Tracy. What's wrong?"

"What was going on in the kitchen with you and Jonathan?"

"Nothing, Tracy. What do you think was going on?"

"I'm asking you straight up instead of drawing conclusions, and I would like for you to tell me the truth."

"I am telling you the truth. I would never disrespect you that way. Not with your friend and not in our home." She then saw the tension leave his body. He relaxed a bit, and his jaw loosened. She breathed a sigh of relief.

"Look, I'm sorry, and I believe you. It's just when I walked in, you looked like I walked in on something you didn't want me to hear. Now, Dr. Warner has told me to confront the issues and ask questions instead of drawing my own conclusions, and I just wanted to know. You say it was nothing then, okay, I believe you."

November was impressed. They were making progress. "Thank you," she said and kissed him.

"I love you," he said. He hugged her.

"I love you, too."

Chapter Thirty-two

"Tracy, you check it. I'm too nervous to look," November said.

He got up off the side of the tub, went to the sink, and picked up the stick. "It says pregnant," he said nonchalantly.

"No way," she said. She gave a little squeal.

"Yes way. See?" He showed it to her, and she screamed. "So, I take it you're happy?"

"And I'll say you are correct, big daddy," she said, and he hugged her.

"Aww, man, another baby boy coming our way." He smiled.

"Man, what are you talking about? This one is going to be a girl."

"I doubt it. I told you the Stones only make boys," he said, sticking his chest out.

"Whatever," she said, slapping his arm. "I can't wait to tell April and Darlene." She looked at the test and grinned.

"Well, if it is a girl, Darlene's gonna be mad," he said.

"And if it is a boy, April gon' be mad," she said.

"Yep. To have four boys and didn't make one girl sucks."

"And look at April. Poor Tony. He has four girls, so he's got it worse." They laughed.

"Well, it don't matter what this one is. I'm gonna be happy."

"Really?"

"Yes, baby, really. Because, after this one, we are having another anyway."

"No, no. Hell, no. This is it."

"What do you mean, Novey? You said we would have three." He followed her into their bedroom.

"Well, I've changed my mind."

"How are you just gon' change your mind?"

"Because, baby, I'm getting older. At the rate I'm going, I'll never be able to start my own business."

"Aww, here we go. I thought we discussed this. I thought we decided it was better for you to stay home and take care of the house."

"No, baby, *you* decided that."

"No, we agreed when we decided to try to get pregnant that you would stay home."

"Not forever, baby. I love you, and I love our son, and I want to be a good mother to our kids, but I don't want all my hard work in school and getting my degrees to be a waste. I'm tired of feeling like a nobody, babe."

"Novey, you're not a nobody. You are a wife and a mother. Don't I give you everything you need? Is this not the house that you wanted? When you wanted to get the Tahoe, I got it for you. When you wanna shop, you shop. You eat wherever you wanna eat. I work hard to provide my family with a good lifestyle.

"I don't want you to stress out like you do when you're working. Having your own business has its perks, don't get me wrong, because we couldn't live like we do if I didn't, but it was hard, baby. I don't want you to worry about working. Just relax, take care of me, and take care of our children, that's it." He rubbed her back.

What he said was right and made sense, but November still wanted to do it. "I know, Tracy, but I just want something for me. I wanna feel like I have accomplished something. I want to be successful doing something I love to do."

"You are successful at what you do. You take care of me and TJ, and you have provided us with a clean and loving home. I love that you get up and cook me breakfast in the morning. When I call and say I'll be home for lunch, you make me a slamming turkey on wheat. When I come home, the scent of your delicious food hits my nose. I like having you here when I come in from work. You make me feel better when I've had a stressful day. You are my helpmate. I take care of things outside of the home, and you take care of things inside of the home.

"I have a clean home and clean clothes, and my son has his mother to look after him. Baby, you need to just relax and enjoy motherhood. Now that we are pregnant again, you need to relax and enjoy your pregnancy. Just like with TJ, we can hire help on the days you don't feel like doing anything. And I'll take care of you like I always have."

Tears rolled down her cheeks. Everything he said sounded great, and she was happy with the luxuries of life that he offered her, but why didn't he understand that she needed something too? He had his businesses and was looking for new opportunities, but he couldn't understand why she wanted to have her own.

She put her head down. It was useless to argue with him anymore. He didn't see for her what she saw for herself. He was dead set on her being a homemaker, regardless of what she said or felt. She wiped her face and rubbed her tummy. She decided not to discuss the matter anymore because it wasn't like she could start her business tomorrow. She just wanted him to support her in starting her own business in the future.

She turned to him and let him hold her while she sobbed. He held her and continued to run down all the positive things about her being a stay-at-home mom. She didn't dispute it or argue; she just went along with what he said like she normally did. She promised him that she'd relax and not let anything stress her out during her pregnancy and she gave him a faint smile. He kissed her on her forehead and left her alone to rest.

She climbed into bed, pulled the covers over her head, and cried until she fell asleep.

Chapter Thirty-three

Oh, my God, November thought, spotting Kendell sitting at a table with a young, beautiful woman. She turned away to try to make sure he didn't see her. Now seven months pregnant, she thought she looked like a beached whale. She tried to pay for her food, grab her bags, and get out of the restaurant quickly, but before she could make her exit, he called her name. He had gotten up and was walking toward her, so she couldn't just walk out like she didn't hear him. She hesitantly turned around.

"November?" he said again.

"Kendell. Hi. How are you?"

"I'm good. How are you?"

"I'm fine," she said, holding her stomach with her free hand.

"That's good. I see you have a stranger aboard?"

"Yes. She is due in June. I've got about two and a half more months."

"Wow, that's good. How is your son? I know he is getting big."

"Yes, he is, and he's a handful. How is business for you?"

"Business is awesome, thank God. I'm working harder since you've been gone."

"Yeah, I know it's tough."

"Yes, but I manage. I take it you and Tracy are doing well?"

"Yes, we are fine. And your lady friend?" The woman at the table was staring her up and down.

"Well, you know me. I'm still looking for my November, and trust me, she is not it. When I drop her off tonight, she definitely will not be seeing me again." They laughed a little.

November knew she needed to make an exit. Seeing him again and looking into his eyes made her feel some old feelings and she didn't want to go there. Kendell was looking even better than he did back then, and she didn't want to revisit the past.

"Well, Kendell, I gotta run," she said, holding up her takeout. "I've got to get home."

"Okay. It was so good to see you, November."

"You too, Kendell."

He smiled at her. He was gorgeous, and although she loved Tracy, Kendell was a man she could see herself with.

"Take care," she said and headed out the door.

He came out behind her and called her name.

"Shit," she said and turned her attention back to him.

"I just wanted to tell you, November, that I'm honestly happy that you and Tracy worked things out. All I wanted for you was you to be happy. I was sore about the way things turned out, but I'm wise enough to know that you can't go around falling in love with another's man wife. You have to know that I regret the entire situation, but I don't regret meeting you. And I enjoyed working with you."

"I am sorry too, Kendell, that you got mixed up in my and Tracy's drama. I am glad to have had the opportunity to work with you. You are brilliant, and I wish you luck."

"Thank you, November, and when you decide to step out there and give me some competition, call me if you need some help getting things going. I've been through this entire process, and I can help you avoid some of the same beginner business mistakes I made."

"Thanks, Kendell. I'll keep that in mind. Good night." She turned and headed for her SUV.

"Good night to you, November," he said.

She didn't look back. She climbed into her truck and put her bags on the passenger's seat.

She took a few cleansing breaths and closed her
eyes, trying to shake the image of Kendell out
of her mind. She thought about how they used
to hang out and how good he was to her. She
wondered what her life would have been like
if she had fallen for Kendell and gone through
with what Tracy tried to set her up to do.

Her baby moved, and she touched her stomach and shook the thoughts of Kendell off. She
cranked her truck and pulled out and left her
thoughts in the parking space.

Chapter Thirty-four

November sat in the nursery rocking her newborn daughter, Trinity. She looked at her infant and wondered how she and Tracy had made someone so perfect and beautiful. TJ was a handsome little guy, but Trinity had stolen her heart.

She hummed and rocked her little girl, wondering who she would grow up to be. What kind of example would she set for her little angel? She wanted Trinity to grow up knowing how to be self-sufficient and take care of herself. Although November had a good husband who was financially set, it may not be that way for Trinity.

"I'll have to teach you that we women have to be independent and not rely on others to do for us, because we sometimes have to do for ourselves," she said to her two-week-old princess.

November knew she had plenty of time to mold Trinity, but she wondered what example being a housewife set. How would she show her baby girl that she could accomplish anything if she hadn't accomplished the one thing she wanted to accomplish because she was letting someone hold her back?

"Mommy is gonna go for it and do what I gotta do to have some of what I want for myself, so you, little one, will have a role model in your life who at least went for her dreams."

She laid her sleeping baby in her crib and stood there for a few moments with a smile on her face. She was so proud to be the mother of two beautiful children. Her daughter had given her a sense of completion. She loved her husband and was glad to have a man in her life who loved her and was there for her and her children. Tracy wasn't perfect, and he had done things in the past, but by the grace of God, they had made it through. Her family was intact.

Now, there was nothing else to do but prove herself. She knew Tracy was never going to give in to her starting her own business, so she was going to take matters into her own hands. She would just have to show him that she had what it took to be a mother, housewife, and career woman. She was dead set on doing what she wanted to do. Why he couldn't just help her and support her was a mystery to her. If she wanted it, she had to go and get it.

***

"What's so hard?" she asked Jonathan. She gripped the phone tightly. "All I need is a closing date. It is getting more and more difficult to keep this from Tracy. I'm running out of excuses to meet with you and the contractors every other day. You know how my husband is," she said impatiently.

She had found a building and bought the space. It was in a great location, but it hadn't been used in more than eight years, and it needed some major upgrades before it would pass inspection. They were already three weeks behind schedule.

"I know, November, but with construction, you know they run into delays. The more they've worked, the more things they've found that need repair. You knew when you bought the place it was a risk and a time capsule."

"Listen, Jonathan, I know what you're saying, but I'm going broke," she huffed. Tracy had no idea she was using the money Kendell paid back for her business. No way could she dip into their account without him seeing it. "This is the company you referred me to, and you promised they'd make it happen. I want to still have my husband when this is over. Lying to him is horrible enough. I'm tired of sneaking around behind his back."

"I know, November, and I promise you that I'm on it."

"Okay, Jonathan. I'm depending on you to come through for me because if I keep this routine up, my husband is going to find out. I want to be the one to tell him. I don't want him to kill me, do you understand?"

"It's gonna be soon, trust me," Jonathan said.

"I hope so because this is my life we are talking about. I have a lot riding on this. If this doesn't go as planned, things will be bad, and I can't have that happen." She loved Tracy and hated going behind his back doing what she was doing. This had to come to an end before he found out what she had been up to behind his back.

"I hear you, November. Please relax. I will get some answers and dates for you."

"Okay, Jonathan. I'll talk to you soon. And please, if I don't pick up, leave me a message."

"I know, I know," he said.

"Okay, bye," she said and hung up.

Tracy rushed down the steps and into the kitchen. His heart pounded, and he was shaking. He grabbed the scotch and poured himself a shot. He downed it, poured another one, and downed it too. His worst nightmare had come true. November had actually gone out and had an affair. He'd heard it out of her own mouth when he walked past the office. After she had promised him and swore she'd never do it, she did. His eyes welled, but then he heard her voice behind him, and he straightened up.

"Hey, babe, what do you want for dinner tonight?" she asked casually.

He wondered how she could come downstairs and act so naturally and innocent when she had just gotten off the phone with her lover. He didn't face her at all as she moved around the kitchen.

"Tracy, baby, did you hear me? What you wanna eat, baby?"

He took a deep breath. "I'm good. I'm not too hungry." He walked out of the kitchen into the family room.

"Tracy, are you all right?" she asked him. "You look upset, baby. What is it?"

"I'm fine," he said, trying not to look at her.

"Are you sure?" she asked as she put her cell phone into her purse.

"Yeah, baby, I'm good."

"Well, let me run up and check on the baby, and I'll be right back down."

When she ran up the steps, Tracy hurried over to her purse and retrieved her cell phone.

He scrolled through her calls and saw outgoing and incoming calls to and from Jonathan. He almost passed out when he saw Kendell's name. Confused and outraged, he dropped the phone back into her purse and went into the bathroom. What in the hell was she doing talking to Jonathan? And Kendell, for that matter?

He started to feel sick. He wanted to cry and punch the wall at the same time. Who was she actually messing with? Was she sleeping with both of them?

Tracy didn't know what to do at the moment. He didn't know if he should confront her and demand the truth or if he should get more evidence. He let his tears fall. What would possess November to do this? They had a four-month-old baby, and she was sleeping with another man?

He turned on the water, splashed it in his face, and leaned against the sink. When he heard November call him, he dried his face, and he walked out to meet her.

She had pulled out a tube of lipstick and her compact, and she began to apply the makeup. "I'm gonna run and get some takeout. I know you said you were good, but I'm hungry, baby."

He wondered why she was putting on lipstick to do that. "I'll take you," he volunteered.

"Why? If you take me, we'll have to take the kids." She put her makeup back into her purse.

"I don't have a problem with taking the kids, so why do you?" he asked with attitude.

"Because it is October, baby, and I don't think we should take them out in the cold just to get something to eat."

"Well, they've got coats. Get Trinity, and I'll get TJ, and we'll all go."

November didn't argue. When she came back downstairs, she had put the baby's coat and hat on and bundled her in a pink blanket. He and TJ were already ready.

They went to a Chinese restaurant, and on the way back, November reached over and grabbed his hand. He held it and rubbed her diamond. He wondered if she wore her rings when she was with her lovers or if she took them off. His eyes burned at the thought of her cheating on him, but he held his tears in.

When they got home, they sat down to eat. Tracy barely touched his shrimp egg foo young. He nodded and gave her short answers because his mind was all over the place. Finally he trusted her and tried to live like a normal husband, and she'd been doing exactly what he'd expected she'd do.

After they were done, he took the kids up, and November went up behind him. He put the baby in her crib and took TJ into the bathroom to give him a bath.

"Tracy, are you okay, baby?" she asked.

"Look, November, stop asking me if I'm okay. I said I'm fine."

"I know what you said, Trey, but I can tell something is bothering you. At dinner you were short, and you barely ate, and you won't look me in the eyes. So spill, baby. What's wrong?" she pressed.

"I'm fine, November." He continued to bathe his son, without looking in her direction. November stood there for a moment or two, and as she was getting ready to walk away, he spoke. "We are okay? I mean, if we weren't okay, you would tell me, right?"

"Yes, baby, everything is fine."

"You told me before, November, that you'd never lie to me and I trusted you. I want to trust you, but lately you've been acting strange," he said.

"Baby, I know, and I am sorry. I've just been under a little stress, but we're fine."

"Well, what has you stressed out? Nothing's different, so I'm not sure what could be bothering you."

"It's just the change. Trinity is demanding, and TJ is into everything, so my days are full, but I'm okay."

"And you're sure that we are okay? Aside from the children, Novey, are we okay? Because I feel like we aren't okay. If the kids are too much, we can let Rose come back to help out," he said, taking TJ out of the tub.

"Yes, maybe Rose should come back and help out. But you and I are okay, babe. We are fine."

Tracy didn't believe her. He knew what he heard, and he just wanted her to tell him the truth. He walked past her and took TJ into his room and put on his pajamas. He put on a movie for him and told him that he'd be back to tuck him in.

He went down the hall and into their bedroom. November was in the bathroom. He sat on the bed wondering what he should say to her. He waited for her for a few minutes, and when she didn't come out of the bathroom, he went downstairs and poured himself a drink. He would have to get proof because she wasn't going to confess.

Pain and disbelief ran through him, and he thought back to the day he had asked Kendell to seduce his wife. How foolish he had been to have a man go after his wife to see if she'd cheat on him.

Strange. Back then, she didn't cheat, but now, after things were better and perfect for them and their family, she decided to do it?

Not knowing what to do, he closed his eyes and asked God to give him strength. He had to figure out what was really going on. Even though it would be painful, he would rather know than not know.

Chapter Thirty-five

A week had gone by, and November had stayed away from the construction site, trying to handle as much business over the phone as she could because Tracy was going into his jealous moods again. He called her every five minutes and checked on her fifteen times a day. The questioning at dinner was back, and she knew it was because of her sneaking around with her business project. She had to slow down before he figured out what she was doing.

She finally had a completion date. In only three weeks, all of the madness would be over. She was excited and nervous because it was finally a dream come true for her, but she still had to convince Tracy. She still had to show him that she could do what she had set out to do. She wished he had been on board from the beginning, but he had forced her to do it on her own.

She had reserved a room at the Hilton Garden Inn to do interviews. She couldn't do them at the new office because it was still too chaotic. It was not a quiet place where she could talk to prospective employees.

Her cell phone rang when was on the Dan Ryan. She cringed when she saw it was her husband. She hadn't told him she'd be out that day and she knew she had to have a good excuse to be out of the house so early.

"Hey, baby," she said when she picked up.

"Hey, you. Where are you? I called the house like three times."

"Oh, I'm on my way to the store," she said, coming up with the first thing that came to mind.

"Oh, yeah? Why so early?"

"Well, I suddenly had a craving for bagels, so I decided to run out and get some. And some strawberry cream cheese," she said, still lying.

"Oh, yeah, bagels and cream cheese do sound good. How about I meet you at the house in about thirty minutes? I think I wanna take the day off and hang out with you."

November's heart thumped. She had already dropped off the kids at her sister's, and her first interview was in less than an hour. "Well, baby, I had other errands to run, and I am supposed to meet Angela today about noon downtown to have lunch with her. She has been trying to get with me for a few weeks, and I finally told her I'd do it today." She hated lying to him.

"Well, I would like for you to call Angela and tell her not today, because I want to be with you, Novey. It's not often that I can free up some time and play hooky from work. Today, I have some free time, and I want to spend it with my wife."

"Listen, baby, I hear you. And I want to spend time with you, but I've been putting Angela off, and I'd hate to cancel on her."

"Oh, you'd rather disappoint your man than tell your girlfriend you can't make it?"

"Tracy, it's not like that, baby."

"Oh? Well, tell me, November, what is it like, then? It is obvious that your plans are more important than me. Or are you on something else besides meeting your girlfriend?" he asked, and November knew where their conversation was going. She would just have to reschedule everything. She didn't want to upset her husband.

"Okay, baby," she said. "Listen, having lunch with Angela is not important, okay? I am gonna call April and take the kids to her. I'll meet you at the house in a little over an hour, okay? Just give me time to drop them off and go to the store, my love. Then I'm all yours." She hoped she sounded convincing.

"Okay, November, I'll see you in a while. I love you."

"Okay, baby. I love you too," she said and hung up.

She dialed Kendell quickly. The kids were already dropped off, so she just had to get her interviews taken care of. When she got him on the phone, she begged him to go down and take care of them for her. At first, he said no, he couldn't make it, but after she explained her dilemma with Tracy, he agreed to do it, and he told her she owed him big time.

She got off the expressway and headed back toward her house. She stopped at the grocery store and got the items she told her husband she went out to get. She went home, and then she took off her suit. She had just washed the makeup off her face and was trying to look natural when he walked in the door.

"Hey," she said.

Tracy looked at her suspiciously. "Hey," he said and went over and kissed her. He held her for a moment, and she could feel him shaking.

"Tracy, baby, what is it? What is bothering you? You've been acting so weird lately, baby. What's up?"

He looked at her for a moment or two before he spoke. "Tell me the truth, November. Are you having an affair?"

She took a step back and put a hand to her chest. "No, Tracy, no," she said.

"November, don't lie to me. I overheard you—" Her cell phone rang, and he stopped talking.

From where it was on the counter, they could see Kendell's name on the screen. November wanted to pass out. She stood there and watched it ring.

"Answer it, November. Don't mind me. I'm just your husband." There was fire in his eyes.

"Tracy, baby, it's not what you think. It's nothing like that, I promise."

"Then answer it, November!" he yelled. It stopped ringing. "You said you would never cheat on me, Novey, and I believed you. I've been trying to fix our marriage and get help for us, and then you do this."

"Tracy, baby, please. I'm not cheating on you. I'm not messing with Kendell."

"Then why in the hell are you talking to him, November? And Jonathan. Why is his number in your damn phone? Tell me that!"

That caught her off guard. "Huh? What?" she asked. She wondered how he knew she had been talking to Jonathan too.

"'Huh? What?' Don't play games with me, November." He walked over to his briefcase and pulled out some papers. "I went online and printed the bill, so don't fucking lie to me."

"I can explain," she said, stuttering.

"Explain what, Novey? Which one are you fucking? Who were you on your way to fuck this morning, Jonathan or Kendell?" His nose flared and his fists were clenched.

"Tracy, how can you say that to me? It's nothing like you think, baby, I swear. I was going to tell you, but I wanted to surprise you. You've gotta believe me. Come on, baby, let's sit down," she said, trying to grab his hand.

"Don't touch me, November," he said, yanking away from her. "You can't sweet-talk me like you always do. You are a liar. I knew you were no different from Treva. I knew you'd do the same thing." He threw the cell phone bill at her. "And I got your hotel confirmation from your e-mail, too." He went back to his briefcase, took more papers out, and threw them at her too.

He had been going into her e-mail? "Tracy, it was for—"

Tracy sprinted up the steps. She followed him, and he rushed into their guest room and emerged with a suitcase.

"Tracy, are you serious?" she cried, but he walked right past her into the bedroom and tossed the suitcase onto the bed. He unzipped it and flipped it open. She stood there trembling, and he went into the closet. He took things out of the closet to pack.

"Tracy, what are you doing? Aren't you gonna hear me out? Let me explain and tell you what's going on."

"I don't care, Novey. I don't want to hear shit. You can save your lies because I'm not interested." He threw his things in the suitcase, and after two more trips, he zipped it shut and picked it up.

"It's for my business, okay? I was trying to start a business!" she yelled. Tracy paused on his way to the door, and she continued. "I wanted to surprise you. Kendell has been helping me with my advertisement business, and Jonathan has been my Realtor. I swear. Please, baby, don't leave. Please. That's the truth, Tracy. I swear that's what all of this is about," she said, crying. "Just please don't leave. I know I should have told you sooner, but I wanted to surprise you. Please."

"Advertisement?" He raised an eyebrow. "You're going behind my back to build a business?"

"Yes, Tracy, that is my big secret, okay? I know how you felt about me going into business for myself and I just wanted to show you I can do it. That's all, baby. That is it. I am supposed to open in three weeks. Today, I was supposed to hold interviews for my new staff at the Hilton. I wasn't meeting nobody, baby, not like that. I just wanted to show you I could have a business and still take care of you and the kids. I didn't wanna do this behind your back, Tracy, but you were so adamant and so negative. You never considered me and what I wanted. You never supported me on something you knew from the day we met I wanted to do."

"So you go behind my back and think that it would go over smoother if you were already in business, November?" He set his bag down. "How could you keep something like this from me? No way I'd let Kendell and Jonathan do for you what I should have been doing for you. How could you go into something so major without discussing it with me, November? If I had known that you were this sincere and serious, do you honestly think I wouldn't have helped you?"

Her mouth dropped open. He had always been so negative. Every time she brought it up, he'd change the subject or refuse to discuss it. If she had thought he'd help her, she never would have gone behind his back.

"I honestly don't believe you would have helped me, Tracy. I've known for a long time how you feel about this. I didn't want to come to you again and have you shoot me down like you've done in the past. You've never shown interest in me going into business for myself. You always gave me the 'you should be happy here at home taking care of me and the kids' speech, so I had to step out there on my own, Tracy. Trust me, it was a difficult decision for me to do it, but I had to."

"Baby, do you know how much I love you? Do you know how important your happiness is to me? Even if I had been resistant and gone into this kicking and screaming, I would have done it for you, November. I'm your husband. You cannot make decisions like this without me. You were so set on what you wanted that you put your needs before our marriage. That is what I'm angry about right now." He turned and walked out of the bedroom and went downstairs.

November didn't go after him. She decided to let him have a moment before she said anything else to him. When she finally went down, she was relieved that he hadn't left.

"Listen, I know you are upset, Tracy, and I know that you are not just gonna get over this in a few moments, but I want to tell you I'm sorry for lying to you. I know I should have told you, but I was scared. I am sorry."

He didn't say anything at first. "Just leave me alone for a while, please," he said.

She went back upstairs. She didn't know what to think, and she didn't know what else to say. A few minutes later, Tracy came up and handed her cell phone to her. She had another missed call from Kendell. Tracy walked out of the room, and she called Kendell back. She might as well, since things couldn't get any worse.

Kendell told her the interviews went well and he had scheduled second interviews for the candidates she might like. She thanked him for helping her out on such short notice. They talked for a few moments, and she broke down and told him what had happened with her and Tracy.

After she was done, she went downstairs. Tracy was gone. She looked in the garage and saw his truck was gone. She called him, and it went straight to voice mail. She didn't want to cry, but tears burned her eyes. She was right back at square one with her husband. All the progress they had made was for nothing. She may have ruined her marriage behind a stupid business.

Chapter Thirty-six

"I don't know, Doc," Tracy said.

"You have to know, Tracy," Dr. Warner said. "You've been gone almost a week. You have to have an idea of what you want," he told him.

Tracy had pulled another disappearing act on November. He had been so mad when he found out about her secret business that he had just gotten into his truck and left. He checked into a hotel and planned to go home the next day, but when he called November, they argued about him not coming home. It had blown up so bad that he didn't go home another night. Those two nights turned into three, and three into four. He didn't want to spend a fifth night without her.

"I know what I want, Doc, but will it guarantee that I can be stable and trust her? I mean, the last thing I want is to not be with her. I love her. I miss her, and I miss my kids. My life is empty without them, and to start over is not an option. I love November too much."

"Well, then, you know the answer, Tracy."
The psychologist wrote something down on his
notepad.

"I know, but I'm scared."

"Look, we've talked about fears and realities.
The reality is life is going to go on. You will
have good days and bad days. Living in fear
doesn't control the outcome. Whatever is going
to happen is going to happen, Tracy. Nothing
is guaranteed. Life is always going to throw
us a couple curveballs. It's full of what-ifs and
uncertainties, but do you give up and let fear
consume you?"

Tracy remained silent.

"No. You deal with the bad and enjoy the good,
and overall, the good outweighs the bad. You
have to relax your mind and take one second,
one minute, one hour, and one day at a time.
Your marriage is going to take work, trust,
patience, support, understanding, and a million
other sacrifices from you and your wife. If I
could just write a prescription for life, I would be
out of a job because everyone's problems would
be solved. All I can do is advise you and give you
the tools to fight another day.

"You are a man with a family and the choice is
yours. You can either continue to stay away and
never go back, or you can go home, hold your
wife, and tell her you love her no matter what.

Support her in whatever she decides, and even if it doesn't work out, you be there for her and help her get through it. If it's a success, you celebrate with her and tell her, 'Good job.' Either way, you have to be there for not only her, but your two children. Taking it one day at a time."

Tracy finally spoke. "Doc, what if—"

"What if what? You said you'd do anything to save your marriage. The first day you walked into my office, you told me that you'd do whatever it takes to save your marriage, right?"

"Yes, but—"

The doctor shook his head. "But what? What if? Yes, let's answer that question. What if you go home, support your wife, and you live happily ever after? What if you go home and support your wife and her business fails, and you're there to wipe her tears and comfort her and make her feel better? Either way, it's a win-win situation."

Tracy smiled when he thought about it. If he just gave her a chance, she'd be successful. Only if he supported her and helped her. Even if she wasn't successful, she still needed to try it for herself. All he had to do was be there for her. So what she lied? She only did it because he had been against it from day one. It wasn't her fault that he hadn't been supportive.

He had a few things going on, and she'd never told him, not once, to not open another store or chain. She supported him in all things. Even if she thought it was risky, she told him she was behind him, but as soon as she wanted something, he had given her the finger, as if her dreams didn't matter. Even after he pulled that bullshit with Kendell, she was still right there by his side, loving him with all she had. All his wife wanted to do was live out her dream in advertising.

What was so wrong with that? She had come up with all his sales slogans and headliners. She was brilliant. She did have what it took to be successful, and he had to get his head out of his ass, go home, and make things right.

He finished his session with Dr. Warner and headed back to his hotel room. The first thing he did was call Jonathan.

"Hey, Jonathan, this is Trey. What's going on, man?"

"Nothing too much, man." Tracy could hear the question in Jonathan's voice. He sounded nervous.

"Look, man, relax. It's all good. I just have a couple questions for you."

"Sure, man. What's up?" Tracy could tell he relaxed.

"When is my wife's grand opening?"

"Supposed to be in about twenty days. Why?"

"What's left to do?"

"Well, minor things, mostly cosmetic."

"Okay. What can we do to make this happen in, maybe say, ten days?"

"Wow, man. Shit. I'd have to double the staff and have evening hours. That means overtime, and I'm sure that is gon' cost. We are already just a minute away from being over budget."

"That's it?"

"Basically."

"Check this out: I have been a fool. I almost walked away from what matters to me the most. If I can get a night crew, will that speed things up?"

"Sure, man, that would be great."

"Cool. Listen, don't tell November we spoke. Stall her and keep her away from the site. I'll do whatever it takes to open her place in ten days."

"I'm on it."

"Let me make some calls, and I'll call you back."

"Okay, Trey, man. That sounds good."

"A'ight."

"And, Trey?"

"What's up?"

"She loves you, man. Through the whole process, she wanted to tell you."

"I know, man."

"Trey, that woman loves you and values her marriage and those kids. She said over and over again that she'd never let anything come before you guys."

"Jay, man, I know and I'm going home. I am not gonna spend another night away from them. Trust me, I made some bad decisions, and she has been there for me. No way I can't be there for her."

"I'm glad to hear that, my brother. She'll be happy when you do what you need to do. She hasn't counted you out. All she said was, 'He just needs some time.' She never gave up on her marriage or you. It takes a strong woman to still defend you after everything. She still has your back, Tracy."

"I know, Jay. I'm blessed to have her. That is why you have to help me make this happen. I just want her to be happy."

"I gotcha. I'm on it. Just hit me back with the contractor's info so I can get a night shift going. If we can do that, we maybe can pull it off in less than ten days. I'm telling you, what's left is all cosmetic."

"Okay, man. I'll be in touch," Tracy said.

Chapter Thirty-seven

The kids were asleep, and November was on the sofa in the family room. She had on her bathrobe over shorts and one of Tracy's T-shirts. Her hair was tied up, and she had on her wrap cap. She had a Kleenex in one hand and a glass of wine in the other, watching *The Notebook* for the first time, and it had her sobbing and thinking about Tracy. Her eyes were swollen, and her head ached from all the crying.

She muted the volume and sipped her wine. She missed Tracy and wanted him to come back home. She had beaten herself up about going behind his back to open her business. She should have just told him instead of hiding it from him, she thought as she refilled her glass. The idea of having a business was wonderful, but she didn't want it if it meant her marriage.

The last time they talked, they argued, and she had said some evil things to Tracy. It was no wonder he hadn't come home to her that night. She had been mad at first, but after a few days, she calmed down. She just wanted him to come home. If he didn't want her to have the business, she wasn't going to. She would finish the construction on the space and put it back on the market. She just wanted to have peace in her home. She wanted that more than anything.

She was on her way back to the couch, after she put the bottle back into the fridge, when she heard the garage door open. It scared her for a moment, but then she realized it meant her husband was home. She ran to the bathroom and snatched her wrap cap off and combed her hair down. Then she hurried and got her gloss from her purse and put some on her lips. She didn't have time to run upstairs and change, so she made a mad dash to the sofa and sat down just before he came through the kitchen door.

He looked like a ray of sunshine to her. She was happy to see him, but she didn't make any moves. She waited for him.

"Hey," he said.

"Hey," she said back.

After a moment or two, he walked over and sat on the coffee table in front of her. She tried to hold back her smile, but she couldn't, and he smiled back.

"Listen, Tracy, I'm sorry for going behind your—"

"Shhh. No apologies necessary. I've been an asshole."

"No, Tracy, I—"

"No, baby, you listen. I know why you did what you did, and I know how important this is to you. I have no right to hold you back from something you desire in your heart to do. It was not fair for me to not support you or even give you a chance to try. You've supported me in every business decision I've made over the years, and I want to do the same for you for a change. I'm sorry for not listening to you when you tried to tell me time and time again about starting your business."

"Tracy, do you mean what you're saying?"

"Yes. I'm with you one hundred percent."

She froze and her mouth opened wide, but no words came out at first. She blinked and then after comprehension dawned she let out a, "Thank you, baby. I can do this. I know I can do this," with excitement.

"I know you can, baby, and I will be here to help you with whatever. We'll hire Rose full-time to help with the kids, whatever it takes. It is all gonna work out."

She sat up on the couch and came closer to him. She kissed him, and he pulled her closer. They kissed passionately, and he pushed the robe off her shoulders. Her body was ready to take her husband back, so she went for his belt, trying to unbutton his pants.

No matter how bad things got, they always found their way back to each other and had no trouble picking up where they left off. They moved upstairs, and Tracy took control from there.

The next morning, the aroma from the kitchen woke November up. She opened her eyes and looked at the clock. It was a little after ten a.m. She rolled out of bed and went into the bathroom. Her reflection made her jump. Her hair was a mess. She started the water in the shower and used the bathroom before she stepped in.

After cleaning herself up, she put on a fresh robe and went downstairs. Everyone was up, and her man was cooking. Trinity was in the swing and TJ was in his booster seat with Cheerios all over the table.

"Hey, baby. Good morning," Tracy said.

"Hey, why didn't you wake me?"

"Well, you've been with the kids for the past few days, and I wanted to let you get some rest."

"Thank you, babe," she said, and they kissed. "You didn't have to do all this." She pinched a piece of turkey bacon.

"Oh, yes, I did. First, because I love you. Second, because after last night, your man is starving. And Cheerios is not man food." They laughed.

"Well, I can take it from here," she said.

"No, ma'am. You sit down. I got this."

"Okay," she said, not arguing. She poured herself a glass of orange juice and had a seat. A few minutes later, he put a plate in front of her. It looked delicious. He sat down across from her, bowed his head, and said grace.

"Well, my dear, I have a surprise for you," he said, reaching for the syrup for his hotcakes.

"What? What kind of surprise?"

"Well, when you are done, you need to pack, because we are going to Hawaii."

"Hawaii?"

"Yep. You, me, and the kids," he said and put a forkful of hotcakes into his mouth.

"For how long?"

"Ten days."

"Ten days? Baby, the office . . . I open soon. I don't need to be taking any trips. I need to be here in case something happens."

"Listen, baby, it's okay. I talked to Jonathan and Kendell this morning, and they guaranteed me that they can handle everything for us while we're gone."

"You talked to Kendell?" she asked, surprised.

"Yes, I talked to Kendell, and it's all good, baby. Don't worry."

"But, baby—"

"Shhh. Trust me. Now eat. We have to pack. We need this. You, I, and the kids need some Stone family time. Your place still has twenty days, so you'll be back in time to finish up. But we need this."

She smiled. She could use a break from the construction, the noise, and the stress. When she finished her breakfast and cleaned the kitchen, they threw a couple of suitcases together. Tracy told her whatever she forgot or didn't pack, he'd buy when they got there.

After they landed in Hawaii and arrived at their hotel, the kids were asleep. November and Tracy took advantage of their quiet time by taking a bath together. After, they sat out on the lanai enjoying the view and sipping champagne. The mid-October weather was nothing like the weather in Chicago, and they loved the change of scenery. They ordered room service for dinner and ate by candlelight.

"Enjoying yourself, Mrs. Stone?"

"Oh, yes. It is beautiful out here. This has to be a dream," she said, holding Tracy's hand.

"Nope, this is real, my love."

"You know, Tracy, I never thought my life would turn out like this," she said.

"Like what?"

"Like this. You and the kids. I mean, I've always known I'd get married and have kids someday, but it still amazes me sometimes that it happened."

"Well, baby, it's real, and you have a big-headed husband and two big-headed kids," he joked.

"Hey, Trinity's head isn't big," she protested.

"But mine and TJ's are, huh?" he said.

She laughed. "Hey, like father like son, right?"

"Yes, you're right, beautiful, and it's all good. We are blessed with two beautiful children, and I have the finest wife on the planet."

November almost spit out her champagne. "The finest on the planet?" she asked.

"Yep. I know what I said." He gave her a smile.

"And I have the finest husband in the universe," she said.

He burst into laughter. "I can live with that," he said.

"Thank you, Tracy," she said when they finished dinner. "Our marriage is solid, and I am glad you chose me."

"You're welcome. I want to also thank you for forgiving me, and I'm glad you chose me." They toasted. "Now, can we get on to the lovemaking? Because I'm ready." He rubbed his hands together.

She smiled. "You know what? You're nasty."

"I know. And you know you like it."

He eased over to her lawn chair, and he lifted her legs up, put them across his lap, and rubbed them. They got up and made their way back inside and ended up on the huge bed. He kissed her everywhere, making sure he didn't miss a spot on her body. After they were done, he lay with his body wrapped around hers.

"I love all of you."

"Thank you, Tracy. And I love you too."

Chapter Thirty-eight

"Are you sure everything is in order?" Tracy asked Kendell.

He had called while November was in the shower. They hadn't made the ten-day mark, but they were still seven days before the original opening date, and he was anxious to surprise his wife. It had been hell keeping her from the site when they got back from Hawaii. He kept her busy and made sure Jonathan and Kendell helped him to help her relax and stay away.

"Yes, man. Everything is done."

"And everyone will be there, right?"

"Yes, Trey. Man, for the hundredth time, relax. We have done everything you asked us to do. Everything is in order. You just get her there on time."

"I am relaxed. This just means so much to Novey."

"I know, man, and I'm glad you two worked it out," Kendell said.

"Yeah, me too. And thanks, man, for helping me out. I know we've had our issues, but I do appreciate you stepping up and helping my wife. You are a good guy, Kendell, and I can't tell you how much respect I have for you, man. No matter what, you've always tried to do the right thing. Even when I was on some ol' crazy shit, you've tried to do the right thing. Again, I'm sorry for my shit."

"Well, man, your wife is a good girl, and for some unknown reason, man, she loves your ass," he said, and they laughed. "Even if I wanted to, she was yours true blue."

"Well, I do know how to pick 'em," he said jokingly.

"Yeah, well, God had a hand in that, because in all honesty I still don't think you deserve her. But I ain't hating. You make that woman happy."

"Yes, man, I try. But you, Kendell, are a standup guy and I know that we may not be as tight as we were back in college, but I hope that you and I can hang again."

"We'll see, brother. Just take it one day at a time. We all have some healing to do, but right now I gotta get over there and make sure we are still on schedule."

"I feel you, bro, and thanks again."

"Don't mention it. I'll see you guys around two," he said, and they hung up.

Tracy made a few more calls while November was in the bathroom. Everything seemed to be in order. All he had to do was get November in her good clothes and get her out of the house. It wasn't going to be easy because November wasn't the easiest woman to surprise, but he had to pull it off because it was something he could finally say that he was happy for her about. Now that things were in place, the idea of her having her business wasn't a bad idea at all.

Chapter Thirty-nine

"Where are we going, baby, please?" November asked as they rode in his Infiniti. She had a satin blindfold on.

"If I told you it wouldn't be a surprise, now, would it?" he said, taking her hand down from the blindfold.

"Come on, Tracy. I feel ridiculous riding around blindfolded."

"Well, you look beautiful to me," he said rubbing the back of her hand.

"Ha, ha, ha. Now, please can I take this thing off?"

"No, baby. Come on. Let yo' man surprise you."

"I wanna be surprised, Tracy, but I don't wanna ride around with this thing over my eyes."

"Just a little longer, I promise. Okay, baby?" he said, taking her hand down again.

"Man, babe."

"November, come on. It's not that bad."

"Okay, okay. I'll be patient," she said and tried to relax in the seat. She tried to forget how silly she thought she looked by singing with the music on the radio. They slowed, and she was anxious to see what the big surprise was. He parked, and he told November to hold tight while he came around to help her out.

"Can I look now?" she asked before he could get out.

"No. Just wait a few more moments, baby," he said and closed his door. He opened her door, and he took her hands and helped her out.

"Baby, come on. Where are we?" she asked impatiently.

"You'll see," he said and guided her directly in front of her new office building. They stopped, and November couldn't take it anymore. "Okay, are you ready?" he asked.

"Yes, yes, yes. I'm ready. Please can I take this thing off?" she asked, and he gently removed it. She stood there and couldn't believe what was in front of her. Her office was done, completed, and there wasn't a construction worker in sight. "Tracy no, no way, no freaking way. How can this be? I mean, oh, my God," she said looking at the door with the big bow on it.

"You wanna go inside?"

"Yes, yes, I wanna go," she said shaking. He held her hand, and they walked up to the door.

He opened it, and she walked in first. "Oh, my goodness. Oh, my goodness," she said looking around. It was amazing.

"Come on, there is more," he said grabbing her hands. They walked around the entire building before going into her office. When she got to the office door, Tracy stood back, and she rubbed her hand across her nameplate. When he opened the door, she almost had a heart attack when everyone yelled surprise.

"Oh, my God," she said and started to cry. She was overwhelmed and couldn't believe that she finally had her own agency. They popped open a bottle of champagne and filled everyone's glass. They had to open more than one bottle because everyone was there including November's parents.

"I'd like to make a toast to the most brilliant, talented, and beautiful woman I know," Tracy said. "Mrs. November Shareese Stone. I'm so proud of you, baby, and I wish you more success than your opponent Kendell Gordon, who's going to be needing a job when you blow every other advertising company in Chicago out of the water," he said, joking, and they all laughed. "I'm a better man today because of you. Congratulations, my love," he said, and everybody clinked their glasses.

"Speech, speech, speech," everyone yelled.

"Wow, y'all. I wasn't prepared for this, and I . . . I can't began to say how happy this makes me. I am so blessed to have family and friends to love me so much and be there for me like everyone has. Jonathan and Kendell, thank y'all so much for putting up with me when I was stressing out of my mind with business and my personal issues. Y'all been there for me, and I wanna say thanks, guys. Thanks to my parents for just encouraging me when I thought no one cared. And, April, you've been wonderful to me keeping my kids when I had to run all over the place. Tracy, I know we've had it rough, but I'm glad that we are where we are today, and that's together. I've learned that we can accomplish anything as long as we are together.

"To my new staff, I look forward to working with you guys, and we are gonna kick some butt; however, Kendell, don't worry, because we may be the last two agencies standing," she said and winked at him. "I just want everyone to know that this is just the beginning of the best days of my life and I am so happy to be able to share this with you. Again, thank you, everyone," she managed to say without crying.

They ate, drank, and acted as if they were in a club celebrating. After everyone was gone and the place was all cleaned up, Tracy locked the door after the cleaning crew and catering service.

November exhaled. "Wow, what a day," she said.

"Yep, but a good one."

"You can say that again."

"So, how do you feel, Mrs. Stone?" he asked pulling her into his embrace.

"Like I'm the luckiest woman on earth. I mean, everything I wanted and dreamt of is now reality."

"Well, good things take time, and all I see in your future are good things."

"Oh, really? How can you be so sure?"

"First, because you are an extraordinary woman. You are a good mother and a perfect wife. Nothing but good things are in store for you, and I'm going to be right there with you all the way. I got your back one hundred and ten percent."

"Well, my dear, I plan to hold you to that," she said, and they kissed.

"Now that we are all alone, Mrs. Stone, how about we break in this here office like we broke in our new house?"

"Oh, yes, that's what I'm talking about," she said, and they made love in every room in the building.

On their way home, they exchanged glances and knew that, from that moment on, they were unbreakable and there was absolutely nothing they couldn't survive. Love cured it all.

The End